"It's always somet...
never get any time...
time."

Sam put her arms around his neck and kissed his lips lightly. "I guess I'd better go in and brush this hay out of my hair before my father gets home."

"That's just what I mean," said Pip. "If it's not one thing, it's something else. Look, Sam, we love each other, right?"

She answered him with another kiss. She could have kissed him for hours, but he held her tightly and began to speak.

"So why don't we go away together for the weekend, huh?"

Books by Janice Harrell

Puppy Love
Heavens to Bitsy
Secrets in the Garden
Killebrew's Daughter
Sugar 'n' Spice
Blue Skies and Lollipops
Birds of a Feather
With Love from Rome
Castles in Spain
A Risky Business
Starring Susy
They're Rioting in Room 32
Love and Pizza to Go
B.J. on Her Own
Masquerade
Dear Dr. Heartbreak
The Gang's All Here
Your Daily Horoscope

JANICE HARRELL earned her M.A. and Ph.D. from the University of Florida, and for a number of years taught English on the college level. She is the author of a number of books for teens, as well as a mystery novel for adults. She lives in North Carolina.

JANICE HARRELL

Your Daily Horoscope

Keepsake FROM
CROSSWINDS

CROSSWINDS

New York • Toronto • Sydney
Auckland • Manila

First publication November 1988

ISBN 0-373-88036-7

RL 4.9, IL age 11 and up

Dear Reader:

Welcome to our line of teen romances, Keepsake from Crosswinds. Here, as you can see, the focus is on the relationship between girls and boys, while the setting, story and the characters themselves contribute the variety and excitement you demand.

As always, your comments and suggestions are welcome.

The Editors
CROSSWINDS

Chapter One

Samantha was minding her own business the day it all started. She was waiting in her father's car in the Nashua County High lot and since it was a warm September day she had dangled her legs out the open car door to catch some sun. It was a little tricky to read that way, but she found that if she leaned back far enough she could keep the book in the shade while keeping her legs out in the sun. Not that it was exactly comfortable.

She sneaked a look at her legs to see how they were coming along—she hoped that wasn't a freckle emerging on her knee—then returned to her reading. Mrs. Hutchins had said that they should try to relate what they read to their own experiences and Sam was doing her best to figure out what Wordsworth's infatuation with some Victorian lady had to do with life as she knew it at Robert E. Lee High School. Suddenly she felt a tug at her skirt and glanced up to see a goat nibbling delicately on the hem. She let out a shriek and sat up smartly. Her textbook slid from her limp fingers to the asphalt of the parking lot. "Baa," the goat commented. After a moment's consideration, the goat scrambled into the back seat.

It nuzzled one of the broad leaves of her mom's philodendron, then took a bite. "Stop that!" yelled Sam. The goat showed no sign it had heard her. Sam wondered whether if she took the plant up into the front seat the goat would leap over the seat after it and land in her lap, which would be awful. Or it might bite her, which would be worse. She leaned over the seat and fluttered her hands ineffectually at it. "Go away," she said. But it was finishing off one broad leaf and paused only a second to lick its lips before beginning on the next. It was a small black goat with little horns budding from its head and a swellingly round belly. Under other circumstances she might have thought it was cute.

In the distance she could hear people yelling, but her immediate problem was that her mother's prized philodendron was disappearing. She picked up a flattened paper cup off the floor of the car and held it under his nose. "Nice paper cup," she wheedled, "extra tasty." The goat took a bite of the paper cup, but it returned at once to the philodendron.

Suddenly Sam realized that a herd of boys in football uniforms had surrounded the car. She wheeled around in her seat in a panic.

"This is a Rebel car," someone yelled. "They're trying to kidnap Grogan!"

"No!" Sam protested. "I'm not trying to kidnap him. He just came over here and jumped into the car!"

The face of a huge boy sneered at her through the windshield. He looked as if he had muscles in his neck. "And you just happened to be over here in our parking lot, huh?" he growled. "Some story. You ought to have covered up your Rebel sticker if you wanted us to believe it."

"Can't you see it's a faculty parking sticker?" Sam wailed. "I'm waiting for my dad to come out of a meeting."

One of the boys had come around to the door and had begun tugging on the goat's back legs. "Baa," the goat bleated loudly.

"Watch out for its hooves, Deever," someone warned.

Sam got out of the little two-door car and flipped the lever to make the seat go forward so that the boy would have more room to get at the goat. Then she bent over to pick up her English book and looked around nervously at the huge boys who were gathered around her.

"We're going to have to teach you Rebels a lesson," someone said.

"Bunch of cowards," snarled another kid, "sending a girl to do their dirty work."

"What seems to be the trouble?" said a deep voice behind them.

Sam couldn't remember ever having been happier to see her father.

"Dad, would you explain to them the dumb goat just climbed in our car and that I did not come over here to kidnap him?"

Her father took the pipe out of his mouth. "Kidnap him?" he asked. "Am I supposed to be in on the plot, boys?"

"No, sir," said the guy with short hair, shuffling his feet. The boys stood looking at Sam's father a little shamefaced. Deever had succeeded in getting a collar and leash on the goat and had pulled it out of the car.

"What happened?" asked Sam's father. "Did the goat get out of its pen?"

"You told me you locked it, Turner," someone said.

"Well, I did. But anyway it's not my job to feed him. Benson was supposed to do it."

Sam got into the car, slamming the door closed after her. She was glad to put the car door between herself and the mob outside.

Her father slid in behind the wheel. "You boys are going to have to keep a closer watch on that animal," he said. "We don't want him to wander out on the highway and get hurt."

"Yes, sir," said a blond boy.

"Give my best to Coach Brown, will you?"

As they drove out of the parking lot, Sam shivered. "What creeps! They were really trying to scare me. And they did, too. Did you see them? Subhumans, all of them. No signs of intelligence, and did you see those beady eyes? *Nothing* could make me come over to this school again. It couldn't be more plain that civilization stops at the Fenterville city limits. Why did you have to come way out here in the boonies for your dumb meeting anyway? What was it about?"

Sam's father took the pipe out of his mouth. "It was about improving student relations between our two schools," he said. "The faculty wants to make sure that the rivalry about the Nashua-Fenterville game doesn't get out of hand. I don't have to tell you what happened over at Parkerton last week."

"I don't think anybody around here is planning a riot like the one they had at Parkerton, Dad."

"I hope not. And I would like to point out that those boys were not subhuman, Sam. Please don't go spreading the word that you were surrounded by a mob at Nashua High."

When they pulled in the driveway at home, Sam saw her mother getting out of her own car carrying a carton of milk.

"Did you remember to pick up my philodendron at the nursery?" she asked them.

Sam's mother's philodendron had been carted over to the nursery for treatment of its spider mites. Unfortunately it was all too apparent that spider mites would never trouble it again. Glancing in the back seat, Sam saw that only a couple of ragged stems protruded from the green plastic pot. "There's just a little problem with that philodendron, Mom," she admitted.

Her mother peered in the car window. "Oh, no!" she gasped. "What happened to it?"

"I know you're not going to believe this," said Sam, "but it was eaten by a goat." She glanced at her father. "An agent of the Nashua High Wildcats, actually. But Dad wants us to be cool."

Before school the next morning, Sam was sitting on the edge of the senior fountain with Marcy. "Those guys were animals." She shuddered. "There were hundreds of them bunching up around me. Humanoids—bulging muscles in their necks, bony ridges over the eyes."

"Sort of an *australopithecus* effect," suggested Marcy.

"I guess, but I don't think they dragged their knuckles on the ground or anything," said Sam, trying her best to be fair.

Marcy was not listening anymore. She was watching Luke as he came over to them, and Sam had to admit that he was worth looking at. He was gorgeous, with corn silk blond hair and the bluest of eyes. It occurred to her that if he had been turned into marble he would have made the perfect centerpiece for the senior fountain. He had the straight nose and the softly disordered hair you were always seeing on statues. Only his frayed blue jeans and his smelly sneakers kept him from looking like a work of art. Marcy brushed her dark bangs out of her eyes and slid over to make room for him.

Sam could not quite get used to the intense looks that passed between Marcy and Luke these days. She wanted them to be happy, but did they have to sit there gazing into each other's eyes until they got all gooey around the edges? It put such a damper on conversation. You didn't feel you could go on chattering about goats when people were looking at each other that way.

Marcy finally broke the silence. "Want to hear about how Sam was mobbed at Nashua High and lived to tell the tale?" she asked Luke.

"Are you serious, Sam?" Luke asked. "Did those guys really threaten you?"

"Well, they didn't hurt me or anything, but they seemed to have the idea that I was trying to kidnap their dumb mascot. Actually it just butted its way right into the car and started eating Mom's favorite plant. The next thing I knew, this mob—" She hesitated a second, remembering her father's warning. "Well, anyway, this large group of guys in football uniforms were all around me."

"So it jumped in your car all by itself, huh?" said Luke. "Sounds like a very friendly goat." His blue eyes were taking on the look that Sam had learned to know and distrust.

"Don't go getting any ideas, Luke," she warned.

Marcy punched Luke. "We're seniors, now. We've got our dignity to think about. You're not getting any crazy ideas, are you?"

He shrugged. "Nah. Not me. This year I'm going straight. No trouble. Scout's honor." The bell went off and all around them kids began surging up the front steps toward the doors of the building. Out on the sidewalk some guys had locked arms and were chanting, "Nashua, Nashua, Nashua stinks."

A clutch of giggling girls wearing blue-and-gray beanies passed Sam. The Nashua-Fenterville game was weeks away but despite the efforts of her father's committee, it was easy to see that feelings of rivalry were already heating up.

As she walked up the front steps, Sam found herself scanning the crowd looking for Pip even though she knew she wouldn't find him. He was out of town and wouldn't be back until tomorrow.

Then she caught her breath as she saw him fighting his way against the current of kids to get to her. A moment later he had reached her and put his arm around her. He was so close she could catch the faint warm smell of his hair. She looked up at him and gently touched the Band-Aid on his neck.

"I thought you were supposed to be in Amherst," she said. She hadn't meant for it to come out sounding like an accusation.

"I decided to skip Amherst," he said. "It was really Dad's idea, anyway. I don't think I want a small school, so we got the early bird flight back from Boston this morning."

Up till now Sam had refused to confront the fear that she would lose Pip when they graduated, but she realized it had been there all the time like a cold coin inside of her.

She was afraid to ask him what his plans were—she didn't want to know. It was better to go on hoping he would choose a school nearby.

"Miss me?" he murmured in her ear, as kids carrying books surged past them.

"I've been busy," she said. "I've been attacked by this goat, the Nashua County mascot. It tried to eat my skirt."

"The awful thing is, Sam, I can believe every word of it. How you get yourself into these things—"

"I missed you," she said, feeling a sudden catch in her throat. He squeezed her hand, but then she had to turn to go to her homeroom and they were swept apart by the crowd. In the morning navigating the halls at Lee was like forging through a cattle stampede.

Sam managed to squeeze her way past a bunch of sophomores who smelled strongly of bubble gum and found herself envying them. She was not enjoying her senior year the way she had expected. It was true that she was entitled to sit around the senior plaza now, but she got little satisfaction from the privilege. For Sam, worries about the future seemed to hang over the senior plaza like smoke from unseen fires. No matter how much she tried, she couldn't seem to shake a recurring feeling of uneasiness. It was remotely possible, she thought, that she was not quite ready to be a senior.

* * *

That evening Sam's mother insisted on giving her a cooking lesson. Her mother was expecting to leave any day to help Robin when her baby arrived, and she was clearly having qualms about whether Sam and her father would get enough to eat while she was gone. Sam sat on a stool near the counter, not even pretending to pay attention to the instructions. She intended to live on chili until her mother returned. "Mom, aren't those northeastern schools awfully hard to get into?"

"It depends on the school."

"I mean places like Harvard, Yale, Princeton. That kind of place."

"You aren't getting big academic ambitions this late, are you, Sam? Because there's no way we could pay for schools like that even if you could get in."

"The money's not a problem for Pip's family, though."

"Well, no. Pip's family is the sort that gives gymnasiums to colleges, I suppose."

"That would make it easier for him to get in, wouldn't it? I mean, I guess colleges like people who give them buildings and things."

"Naturally. But I don't think Pip would have to give them a gymnasium to get in. Your father told me he was bound to be a Morehead nominee."

"Pip? A Morehead nominee!"

"Andy?" her mother called. "Didn't you tell me Pip was a shoo-in for the Morehead scholarship?"

Her father strolled into the kitchen. "Bound to be," he said, pinching up some grated cheese with his fingers and sticking it in his mouth. "Nobody's got better grades. Except Marcy, of course."

Sam sat on the kitchen stool feeling as if someone had pounded her on the head with a rubber mallet. It was no surprise to her that Pip made good grades. He put in a lot of time with the books, for one thing, and he knew all kinds of things, and his teachers obviously respected him. But she had not realized that he was in Marcy's league.

"Wait a minute!" she said. "If he actually won the Morehead he would get free tuition to State or to Carolina, wouldn't he? He might decide to go to Carolina, then."

"I doubt if the Byrons would let that weigh with them," said her father. "It's not as if money is an issue for them. They'll be looking for the very best school for Pip. Tell you what, Sam, if you want to know what his plans are, why don't you ask him? That'd be the simplest way to find out."

She saw her mother and father exchange a significant glance and realized that they knew what was bothering her as surely as if she had spelled it out in red paint on the kitchen cabinets.

"Not that it matters that much," she said. She picked up the evening paper off the kitchen table and opened it so it would hide her face. The problem with living in a family was that you had no privacy. Her parents didn't seem to understand that she needed to figure out things on her own. They kept watching her expression closely all the time as if they were waiting for the optimal moment to jump in and give her advice. They didn't seem to understand that the problems she had now were too intimate to discuss with her parents. A person did not lay her love life out on the kitchen table for public dissection. Not if she had any self-respect.

Sam frowned at the newspaper. She felt she was at the beginning of her real life, the part that counted. She could picture herself, a slender, gallant figure, alone and independent, standing on a cliff somewhere, watching the sun come up over the Pacific. The only trouble was that without Pip in it, that picture seemed strangely bleak.

She forced herself to concentrate on the print on the page before her and found her sign in the daily horoscope column. "Major changes for Aquarius in the months ahead," it said. "Send $1 in care of this paper for your personal astro-line predictions."

Change, she thought, pinpointing it. That was what she didn't like. Things were pretty good for her now. She wasn't sure she wanted them to change.

She wondered why no one had thought of having a special extended senior year for people like her who weren't ready just yet to let go of all they had.

Chapter Two

Pip's white Mercedes was parked back by the Dumpster at Burger King. It was not the most scenic part of the Burger King parking lot, but it was the most private. Pip and Sam had been parked there for some time.

"Pip?"

"Mmm?" he murmured.

"Dad said you're probably going to be a Morehead nominee."

Pip pulled away from her and looked at her warily. "Maybe."

"Why didn't you tell me?"

"Because it might not come off, for one thing."

"No, I mean, why didn't you tell me you made those kinds of grades?"

"You think I ought to go around with a pocket calculator figuring my daily average like Marcy?" He grinned.

"Come on," she said. "Do you think I don't know what goes into getting grades like that? You don't have to tell me—I haven't been Marcy's friend for years for nothing. You expect me to believe that being practically at the top of the class is so insignificant you didn't remember to mention it?"

He hesitated. "Okay, now this is the truth, Sam—I figured I just didn't need for people to know. When I was a kid I got all caught up in making good grades, you know? It was important to me. And it was always 'There goes Pip—he's really smart,' that kind of thing. When we moved here, I decided I'd make a clean break. Some people change their names when they move. I quit being Pip-he's-really-smart."

"You could have told me."

"Good grief, Sam. I don't see why you should care. What difference does it make?"

"Did I ever mention that I spent my formative years in Afghanistan while my parents were in the peace corps?"

"No! Really? Gee, I didn't know your parents were in the peace corps. But now that I think about it, they're kind of that type. They—"

"My parents weren't in Afghanistan," she said impatiently.

"What are you getting at?"

"I was giving you an *example*. You see how it changes your whole idea of me when you find out something like that? Didn't that Afghanistan business make me seem positively interesting there for a minute? Sort of cosmopolitan or something. You see, absolutely everything affects the way you think about a person. Suppose you find out some little old lady is a retired trapeze artist. Maybe all she's doing these days is just weeding her garden, but when you find out something like that it changes your whole idea of her."

"I still don't see it. I'm still me. You're still you. How can my grade point average change anything?"

Pip could be amazingly dense about some things. Didn't he see that this news made him seem farther away? It made him seem more like the kind of person who would be snapped up by some fancy northeastern college and never seen in Fenterville again.

"I don't know," she said in a small voice. "Maybe it doesn't make any difference."

"What's the matter, Sam? What's eating at you?"

"Do you catch yourself thinking all the time about the future?"

"Nope. The future seems so far away and we're right here."

"That's very healthy of you," said Sam.

"Thank you," he said, putting his arm around her.

"But don't you ever think about what you want to do with your life?"

"I sometimes think I might like to go into politics. You know that. I might try to get a job as a congressional aide after I get out of school. Of course, if Dad gets anywhere in his bid for governor, that would open up some possibilities, too. It's too soon really to tell. Once I get to college I could get some crazy passion for astrophysics and forget all about politics. You never can tell.''

This would have been a perfect time to ask him which schools he was seriously considering, but Sam's courage failed her.

"What about you?" he asked.

"Seeing the sun rise over the Pacific and riding a camel are biggies for me. I'm really looking forward to getting away from home and being independent," she said. She was disappointed that her voice sounded thin, as if it lacked conviction. The fact was she was not feeling very independent at all at the moment. She was feeling as if she wanted to put her arms around Pip and never let go. "Contrary to what you might think," she went on with determination, "I'm a very independent person."

"Did I say you weren't? What's going on, Sam? Are you mad at me or something?"

Tears began to well up in her eyes. "No, I'm not mad at you," she said. "I love you."

He ran his fingers through her hair and smiled at her. "All right then."

A phone call came in the night the following Monday announcing the arrival of Robin's baby.

"Eight pounds six ounces," Sam's mother said as she shook cinnamon on the toast and prepared to stick it under the broiler. "A good size. And he made nine on the Apgar scale. That means he's very alert, very healthy. Goodness, it's hard to believe I'm a grandmother already, but I like it. It feels good." Steam from the coffeepot had set her mother's hair curling around her temples and her face was pink from the heat of the stove.

She at once launched into a good deal of obstetrical detail, which caused Sam to leap up from her seat and say she guessed she'd shove off to school early.

"You don't want any cinnamon toast?" asked her mother in surprise.

"No, thanks," said Sam. "I'm not hungry."

Outside, Sam began scraping the frost off the windshield of her old car. Her stomach rumbled as she thought of the cinnamon toast she had left behind in the kitchen. She really liked cinnamon toast. What was it with older women and delivery-room stories? Her father never felt as if he had to go over every grisly detail of his Vietnam experiences. In fact, even though Sam's mother had told her that he used to have terrible nightmares, he never talked about the war at all. It was an approach to unpleasantness that Sam infinitely preferred.

She threw her books in the back seat and drove off toward school. She had gotten as far as Winstead Avenue when the car made a funny scraping sound as if something vital had dropped off. Then she noticed that smoke was pouring from under the hood. She was not a mechanic, but she knew this was not a good sign.

Sam pulled over, jumped out and lifted the hood. From what she could tell the smoke seemed to be coming from the radiator area mostly and water was dripping from one of the hoses down below the engine. Since flames were not actually leaping from the engine, she judged the car would probably make it the two blocks to a service station. A few fine drops of rain sizzled as they struck the radiator. Naturally it would begin to rain now, she thought. Next would probably come a great flood with all the animals marching in pairs toward some spaceship. Troubles never came singly. She slammed the hood shut then got in and drove to the service station where she could call her mother. Less than five minutes later her mother drove up at Roy's Exxon. She was dressed in her social-worker clothes, a plum-colored suit with a scarf around the neck, and her hair was pulled back into an untidy bun.

"He says it's a blown gasket," Sam reported as she climbed into her mother's car.

"It can't be a blown gasket. We just had the gasket replaced a few months ago."

"Well, that's what they say it is and they can't fix it. It's a major repair and we'll have to take it somewhere else."

"We're not doing any major repairs before payday. You can ride to school with your father for the next couple of weeks. That makes more sense anyway. It's a waste of fuel to drive two cars to exactly the same place."

"Mom, he doesn't leave school until four o'clock! Lots of times later. You know how he is."

"I'll tell you what, Sam. I'll be leaving for Atlanta Wednesday, and while I'm gone you can drive my car. We'll just park yours in the garage until we can have it fixed. Did they think your car could be driven at all?"

"After it cools off, they said they'd fill up the radiator and that it ought to be okay while I drive it a little way."

"All right then, get Dad to bring you by here this afternoon, drive it on home and we'll worry about repairing it when I get back."

After her mother dropped her off at school, Sam immediately looked around for Pip and spotted him under the overhang of the administration building talking to a girl in a blue slicker. Sam thought he looked more like a tennis pro than a budding Morehead scholar. Maybe because his olive skin kept a tan well into winter, it seemed to her that he always brought sunshine with him. Today he made the drizzle seem like some staging error on the part of the management.

He waved to her and she was startled to see that the girl beside him was Happy Chambers. Pip quickly detached himself from her to come over to Sam, but as Sam watched Happy walk away, she wondered gloomily if Pip found that type attractive. A leggy blonde herself, Sam tended to envy curvy brunettes in those dark moments when her self-confidence waned.

"I didn't know that you knew Happy," she said when he reached her. "Not to talk to, I mean."

He shrugged. "I've seen her in science club, that's all. I've tried to keep my distance up till now. Practically the last time I saw her was at that dance last year when she fell to pieces and slapped you. She looks pretty normal right now, though. No signs of violence. I figure it's kinder to act as if we've forgotten all about it."

Sam doubted that Happy would believe for a minute that she had forgotten being assaulted in front of half the school. It wasn't the sort of thing that slipped a person's mind. Sam watched as the figure in the blue slicker disappeared in the direction of the senior plaza. "When did you join science club?" she asked him.

"Few weeks ago. Remember how you always used to tell me I should get out and get to know more people? I've started thinking maybe you're right. I don't want to graduate from here hardly knowing anybody."

When Sam had suggested Pip get to know more people, she had not had people like Happy in mind. She had meant honest, trustworthy people. Male people. A drop of water dribbled down the back of her neck.

"Wait a minute," she said. "I have to check on something." She darted into the office. In front of the office typewriter, Mrs. Smithers was reading the morning newspaper while she drank a cup of coffee.

"Can I just look at something, Mrs. Smithers?" Sam asked, grabbing the paper.

The secretary turned astonished eyes on her as Sam swiftly leafed to the inside section and checked out her daily horoscope. It was just as she had feared.

"The transit of Mars through Libra continues until the 29th and until that date Aquarians may suffer some setbacks. This does not mean they are any less capable. It is simply that these down periods form a natural part of life's rich tapestry."

"Yuck," said Sam, throwing the paper down on Mrs. Smithers's desk.

"Is anything wrong?" asked Mrs. Smithers.

"Only my life!" cried Sam.

"What were you doing in there?" asked Pip when she joined him again outside.

"Just checking my horoscope."

"You don't believe in that stuff, do you, Sam?"

"Of course not," she said shortly.

"I think this school spirit business is getting out of hand," said Pip. "Look! Blue-and-gray beanies everywhere." She saw that he was right. Large numbers of kids in felt beanies could be seen milling about on the front steps of the school. "I don't see how people can make themselves come to school wearing those things," said Pip. "They look awful."

Sam had to agree that the people wearing the blue-and-gray beanies did look dippy. "It's the Fenterville-Nashua game," she said. "People are flipping out."

She explained to Pip about her father's work on the faculty committee.

"Then I don't have to worry about you showing up in a beanie, anyway," he said. He smoothed her damp hair with his hand. "That's good."

Looking up at him, she found herself thinking about her older sister. One day Robin was announcing she was in love and then in quick order had followed marriage and a baby. It was like a sliding board, she thought, where you suddenly came down with a bump at the end. She tried to imagine herself having Pip's baby but it just wouldn't come into focus. It seemed to make no more sense than the mental picture of her alone on the Pacific cliffs. Maybe you simply couldn't picture the future. Maybe it had to open to you gradually like an unfolding paper fan.

The bell went off over their heads, scattering Sam's thoughts, and she and Pip had to go to their homerooms.

Third period, at newspaper staff meeting, Sam noticed that three staff members were wearing beanies. Game fever was in the air, all right.

"I'm not saying you all aren't turning in a lot of good work," Luke was saying as he paced in front of the blackboard crumbling chalk in his fingers, "but I wish we could get some hard news coverage. We can't run this paper on features alone."

Sam was not paying close attention. She was staring at Happy, thinking that there was no one she distrusted more. Why had Happy been chatting Pip up? And why was she suddenly in the science club? A burning desire to talk about atoms? That didn't seem too likely.

Happy was sitting on the table at the front of the classroom. The table was her favorite perch since it made it possible for her to look down on the other staff members. As usual she was examining her talons. She was obsessed with having the perfect manicure. Sam was convinced she could drive Happy over the edge if she could only lay her hands on a voodoo curse that would produce hangnails.

"Exact-ly what sort of news do you have in mind?" Happy asked Luke, tilting her porcelain nose upward. "We aren't precisely in the center of events of crushing national importance, you know."

"It wouldn't have to be national importance," Luke said. "Something important to us would do, but real news, you see? Not just the usual interviews with new teachers." He looked up to see Jessica beginning to swell with indignation and hastily added, "The interviews we've had have been real good, I didn't mean that. But I just mean we need something to bring the *Traveler* closer to being like a regular newspaper, that's all."

"Cheer up, Luke," said Anita, slumping her ample bulk deeper into the desk. "Maybe we'll have a murder, robbery or suicide we could cover." She stared at Happy. "I'm particularly optimistic about the murder."

"That's enough," said Mr. Perkins, who had been sitting over in the corner marking papers. "I don't like to hear you joking about violence, people. And Luke, you should keep in mind that we do have news coverage. Coverage of student council meetings is news coverage."

"Student council meetings," groaned Kilroy. "What a bunch of junk. I mean, who cares?"

"I think some people could use a little improvement in their attitudes," said Mr. Perkins.

Sam reflected that Mr. Perkins was probably the only person in the world who could look at a boy like Kilroy, with his shaven skull, the fishing lure hanging from his left earlobe, the trademark red elevator shoes with plaid laces and the blue tattoos on his forearms and say that what he needed to change was his attitude.

"I was just hoping we could get a news story that attracted a little more interest than the student council meetings do," said Luke.

"Too bad the Dr. Heartbreak column folded," Happy said, her eyes flickering to Sam's face. "That was popular if nothing else."

Sam gazed back at her with an expression of bland innocence. Happy had no proof that Sam had written the Dr. Heartbreak column that had caused such trouble last year, and if Sam had her way about it she would never get any proof.

"Heartbreak's history now," said Luke. "We've got to look forward. We've got to be innovative. Doesn't anybody have any ideas?"

"One thing people are really interested in," said Reggie, "is this game with Nashua."

"We've covered that," said Kilroy. "We've covered it right down to the pimple on the chin of their quarterback."

"I wasn't talking sports coverage," said Reggie. "I was thinking how at Parkerton they had a riot at one of their games. The fans tore the goal posts down and fifteen people were treated at the hospital. Now that's a news story for you."

"There are laws against inciting a riot, Reg," drawled Happy.

"I wasn't talking about starting one. I was just saying we might get lucky."

Sam was beginning to lose interest in the discussion. Ever since Luke had become editor of the school paper he had chafed continually at its limitations. "Let's cover real news," was his constant refrain, but it never came to anything.

She pulled out her spiral-bound notebook and began a list. She loved lists.

"The stars impel; they do not compel," she printed at the top of the page. That was the motto of "Your Daily Horoscope," and Sam thought it was a good one. To her it meant that she could take control of her own life. A few things jumped to mind at once that she needed to work on.

1. Keep Happy away from Pip (Join science club myself? Voodoo curse?)
2. Keep my car on the road (Auto repair course at community college? Commit highway robbery?)

3. Achieve inner peace and learn to live one day at a time. (Is it possible that this is totally hopeless?)

As Sam glanced over her list she saw at once that some of her options were not very practical. Joining a science club and taking an auto repair course might take up too much time. She was already pretty booked up and adding on more activities might have a bad effect on her grades.

When the bell rang, Sam hung back and trailed after Reggie. "Reg?" she asked. "Do you know anything about voodoo?"

"I'm surprised at you, Sam," he said. "That's a racist remark."

"I didn't mean it that way, Reg, honest! You're always saying that you know everybody and go everywhere, right? I thought you might know somebody that sells little wax dolls or something. Isn't that a pretty basic item? I'm always reading about that kind of thing, but I just don't know any of our local suppliers."

"You want somebody fresh off the boat from Haiti. And I'm not even sure they'd know. Normal folks don't go for that kind of weird stuff."

Sam sighed. She had not been very hopeful about the voodoo anyway. "It's just that I feel like I'd like to have some secret power in reserve just in case I need it," she said, recalling her gruesome horoscope. "I'm worrying a lot lately."

"Yeah, maybe you've got a reason. Danita told me she heard Happy's out for your blood. Something about how she thought you put her boyfriend off of her."

"Great," said Sam. "She's delusional. Just what I need."

"While I got you here, Sam, how'd you like to buy a beanie? Fund-raising effort of the Pep Club."

"No, thanks," said Sam, hastily backing away.

Wednesday afternoon, Sam drove her mother to the Raleigh-Durham airport. "It's been so long since I've taken care of a baby," Sam's mother sighed wistfully. "I just love that new-baby smell they have just at the tops of their heads and their little bitty hands and their exquisite little fingernails."

Sam liked new babies too, in a general way. But what she had noticed about babies is that once you have them, you *have* them. Babies were incredibly permanent. After Sam had had her fill of sunsets and tropical islands, then maybe she would think about babies.

She got out of the car and walked with her mother to the boarding gate.

"Drive carefully on your way home," said her mother. "The roads are so wet. Now, about the house, I think the water heater is fine since we had the new thermostat put on, but I keep all repairmen's cards in the drawer to the right of the sink, so if it breaks down again, just call our regular man."

"All right," said Sam. She stood by expectantly for further instructions of what to do in case of flood, fire, or pestilence, but her mother settled for kissing her goodbye with a worried crease between her eyebrows.

Sam made her way back to the short-term parking lot wondering if finally after all these years she had caught the worrying habit from her mother. Maybe this feeling of doom that hung over her was nothing more than that. Sam's mother could never say anything simple when she left like "Goodbye. Have fun." No, she had to start in with a list of what to do in case anything went wrong. It was no wonder Sam was getting edgy between a lifetime of her mother's worrying, and on top of it reading that horoscope.

When she got back to the car, she realized that she had the most delicious feeling. Her shoulders actually felt lighter. It had to be the feel of freedom.

Chapter Three

Saturday afternoon, Sam, Luke and Marcy were all sitting together on the porch swing. It was like old times except that these days the porch swing creaked heavily under their combined weight. Also they weren't trying to see how high they could make the swing go the way they had been doing in the fifth grade the day the swing chain had broken. Luke's front tooth had been chipped on that long-ago afternoon, but it had since been capped. The smile he gave Sam today showed the full complement of perfect white teeth.

"The reason I asked you to meet me here," he said, "is that I have an idea I want to bounce off of you. But first I want to be sure you've got an open mind."

"Mine is very open," said Marcy, looking at him lovingly.

Sam realized with some misgiving that it was going to be up to her to put the damper on whatever crazy scheme Luke had come up with.

"What about you, Sam?" he asked. "Do you have an open mind?"

"Not really," said Sam. "You'd better go ahead without waiting for my mind to open."

"All I want you to do is look at this clean. Don't think about the past. Don't think about the future. Just consider my idea on its own merits, as if somebody from outer space had put it to you."

"I don't think I'd trust somebody from outer space, either," Sam said.

"Do you have to be so obstructionistic, Sam?" said Marcy. "Let's at least hear what Luke has to say before you go shooting him down."

"I am listening."

"I think we ought to kidnap Nashua's mascot," said Luke.

"I thought your idea would be something like that," said Sam.

"Look at it this way. We want a news story. We've been waiting for years for a real news story, but nothing ever happens we can cover. Now we're seniors and we're down to our last chance. We need to quit sitting around waiting for something to happen."

"You can't just go out and create news," said Sam. "That's your idea, isn't it? That we steal this goat and then we run a banner headline, 'Goat Stolen'? Let me just put it this way, Luke. I don't think that would be in the finest traditions of journalism."

"Okay, I'd be the first to admit it's not perfect. But it's the best we can do. It's an exercise, that's what it is. Maybe we're giving this story a little nudge, but covering it gets us that much closer to the real thing. One gives you the practice for the other."

"Like the difference between a scale and a sonata," Marcy put in.

"Right. Besides, the basic story is there. We wouldn't be making up the rivalry between the two schools. Look around you. Three hundred blue-and-gray beanies sold in a single week. Does this show a ground swell of feeling, or what? We just give it a little focus. By snatching the goat, we make our ordinary background story into sizzling front page news."

"How long do you think we'd have to keep the goat?" asked Marcy.

Sam looked at her incredulously. What had happened to her brain? Had she become some sort of love zombie? Marcy's mental processes had always crumbled a bit when it came to Luke, but this was ridiculous.

"We can't do it," Sam said. "It could be fatal. To me it would, anyway. My father would kill me if he found out about it. He's on this committee for promoting better relations between the two schools."

"How's he going to find out?" asked Luke. "You're always telling me how oblivious he is."

It was true. Half the time her father had his nose in some book. It was her mother who noticed things and her mother was safely away in Atlanta. But there was something else bothering her. She had met the goat. And she had the feeling that anything involving that goat was not going to go exactly as planned. She wished she could show Luke the remains of the phil-odendron.

"You two do whatever you want to, but I'm not going to have anything to do with it. You don't have to worry that I'm going to rat on you because I won't," she assured him. "We'll just pretend this conversation never happened."

"It's not that, Sam. I know you'd never rat, but you've got to help out on this one. We can't do it without you."

"I don't see why not. It's a small goat. Take along a leash. You and Marcy can handle him just fine. If I could just give you one word of advice it would be stay away from its hooves. I wish you the best of luck. I really do."

"But you're the only one of us with a garage," Luke said.

"You're talking about keeping this goat in my ga-rage?" said Sam, aghast.

"Well, nobody ever goes out there, do they?"

"My father's workshop is out there."

"But doesn't he use that mostly in the summer? What's out there now?"

"My broken-down car, all my old bicycles, my baby stroller, things like that," Sam said reluctantly.

"It's a small goat," said Luke. "You just throw down some kitty litter and some hay and you got yourself goat heaven."

"Forget it," said Sam. "Never. Never in a million years."

"Oh, come on, Sam. It's just for a few days," pleaded Luke.

"I don't see what harm it can do," argued Marcy. "And it's not as if we're really stealing the goat. We'd just be borrowing it. People do that kind of thing with mascots all the time. It's practically what mascots are for. It's a great American tradition."

"We can't do it without you, Sam. And you know I'd do it for you," said Luke.

"Sure, you would. I believe you. But that's because you don't have any sense of self-preservation."

"And you know the goat, Sam. I'll bet he'd come to you," said Marcy.

"He ate some of my skirt. That is not exactly a formal introduction."

"It's just for a little while," said Marcy. "Do you have to be selfish about this? Luke just wants the chance to write up one terrific news story, that's all. I'd hide the goat myself if I had anyplace to put it, but I don't."

Sam felt a stab of guilt when she remembered that Marcy sort of lived in a garage herself. Marcy and her mother had lived in straightened circumstances since her parents' divorce. A ratty garage apartment was all they could afford.

"I bet you're worried about what Pip would think," Luke said. "That's it, isn't it?"

"Pip doesn't have anything to do with it," said Sam.

The look that passed between Luke and Marcy dismayed her. They really did believe she had no independence from Pip. It was true that Pip wouldn't like the idea of stealing the goat, but the crucial point was that in this case Sam happened to share his point of view. She couldn't imagine how Luke thought she could hide a goat in her garage. The idea was crazy.

"Come on, Sam. A few lousy days out of your life, the use of part of your garage. Wouldn't you do it just for old time's sake?"

Sam felt her heart contract. It was true that it wasn't such a big thing, really. And how much more time together did they have as a gang? Did she really want to say "count me out"? It was almost like saying she wasn't one of them anymore. Kidnapping the goat would be harmless enough. It wasn't as if Luke were asking her to do anything that was really wrong.

"What would we move him in?" Sam inquired cautiously.

Luke's blue eyes lit up. "My car," he said. "Piece of cake. We get him tonight."

He seemed to think she had agreed to do it. She supposed she had.

Marcy spent that night at Sam's house. At midnight, Luke's car drove up under the streetlight at Sam's corner, paused a moment, then backed up until it was mostly clear of the circle of illumination cast by the light. Sam and Marcy, wearing black turtlenecks and jeans, tiptoed out the front door. Despite their best efforts at keeping quiet, Sam's dog Fruity heard the front door open and began to bark. Marcy froze in her tracks, the whites of her eyes showing all around her irises.

"Come on," said Sam, pulling at her.

"Your father's going to hear him. He's going to get up and check in your room and—"

"No, he's not, either," said Sam. "Fruity barks all the time. Nobody pays any attention."

Meanwhile, in the pantry, Fruity began to bay as if he were witnessing the opening of a grave.

But it was too late now for second thoughts. "Move!" said Sam peremptorily, giving Marcy a shove.

The two girls ran out to Luke's car and jumped in.

Luke accelerated smoothly as he made his way down Mulberry Street.

Marcy licked her lips. "This shouldn't be too hard," she said in a quavery voice. "I was just reading that goats and sheep were among the first animals to be domesticated because they are so easy to herd."

"You haven't met this goat," said Sam.

"The weekend is good for this kind of thing," Luke said. "There's not going to be a soul around out at Nashua. The place is really out in the sticks."

During the drive out to Nashua High, Sam began to wonder if Marcy was right and her father was going to check on her room and find them missing. She had heard him say he never slept as well when her mother was away so it was certainly possible he would get up. She also remembered her mother telling her how when Sam was a baby her father would go into her room several times a night to make sure she was still breathing. When she came to think of it, did she know for a fact that he had discontinued this practice?

"I've got the hay in my trunk," Luke said. "And a couple of huge bags of kitty litter. Everything we need to get him set up in your garage."

It was dark in the car but Sam could hear the excitement in his voice. Luke was never happier than when he was taking some major risk. It was not, in her view, one of his most endearing traits.

At last they drove up in front of Nashua High. The sprawling brick buildings were anonymous dark hulks in the moonlight.

"The pen where they keep him is probably going to be over by the boys' locker rooms," Sam pointed out.

"I see what you mean," said Luke. He drove the car up over the curb onto the grass.

Sam slapped her palm against her forehead. "Did you have to do that? You're going to leave tire tracks on the grass. That way the police will be able to track us down."

"I don't think the police will put all their best people on a goatnapping," Marcy said, shivering a little.

"We've got to drive on the grass," said Luke. "It's the only way to get up close. You don't want to have to drag the goat halfway across the school grounds, do you?"

Sam did not. "Drive on," she said faintly. They spotted the pen as soon as they rounded the main building. It was not directly up against the boys' locker room, after all, but was off near the football field. Sam realized, with some misgiving, that the pen's distance from the locker room might have something to do with the smell it gave off.

Luke drove right up to it and they hopped out, leaving the car headlights shining on the pen. It proved to be a good-size wire enclosure with sides extending perhaps six feet high. Inside the pen was what looked like a doghouse, and beside it a concrete food-and-water trough showed white in the moonlight. Everything seemed to be there except the goat.

"Somebody takes him home with them for the weekend," Sam said, relieved. "He's not here."

"Don't be stupid. Who would want a goat on their hands for the entire weekend?" said Luke.

This artless comment struck Sam speechless.

"I'll bet he's inside that doghouse asleep," Luke went on.

Marcy was rattling the door to the pen. "The door's got a lock," she said.

Hearing the noise of the rattling gate, the goat suddenly appeared. He scrambled out of his little house and came over to Marcy, pushing his nose through the wire sides of the pen to begin nibbling on Marcy's fingers. Perhaps he associated the rattling of the gate with feeding time.

"He seems to be friendly," Marcy said.

"He's just hungry," said Sam. "He's always hungry."

A minute later Sam heard the trunk of the car slam closed and Luke appeared at her side holding wire cutters.

"You keep him interested over there, Marce," he said. "We don't want him to bolt before we're ready."

"He seems to like eating my shirt cuffs," said Marcy.

Luke methodically began cutting the wires. "Okay," he said. "We're ready for him. Let him go."

Sam heard a loud baa.

"Come over here," Luke called. "Good carrot here."

"Have you really got a carrot?" asked Sam.

"Luke thinks of everything," said Marcy.

"You hold the carrot, Marce," said Luke. "I've got to get the leash on. Hey, hold it still! You're shaking the darn thing."

"I hope the police don't keep a watch on this place," said Marcy in a jerky voice. "You know, they must keep an eye out here watching out for school vandalism."

Sam's stomach lurched when she realized that the glow of their headlights was bound to be visible from the highway.

"Okay, that's it," said Luke. "I've got the leash on." But when he pulled on the leash, the goat refused to move. He had dug his hooves into the grass.

"Stop!" said Marcy. "You're pulling the collar right over his head. He's going to get loose."

"Rats!" said Luke. "Sam, get behind him and push."

Get behind him and push. Right. She should have figured that would be her share of the work.

"Why don't I just start backing toward the car with the carrot?" suggested Marcy.

"Great idea," Sam exclaimed. At least that way she wouldn't have to push.

"Only we're going to have to move fast," said Marcy. "There isn't much of this carrot left."

Marcy backed toward the car, then she nervously tossed the butt of the carrot up on the back seat. The goat did not hesitate to leap after it. Sam quickly slammed the door closed behind him.

"All *right*!" exclaimed Luke. "Way to go. Told you it would be a piece of cake."

"Who gets to sit with the goat?" Sam asked.

"I'll get back there with him," Marcy said.

"No, not you, Marce," said Luke. "You're already a bundle of nerves."

"Fear not. I, Samantha, girl of steel, will sit with the goat."

"Don't you think you can handle it, Sam?" asked Luke. "It's just a little goat, some kind of pygmy breed, I expect. It's—"

"Don't tell me, let me guess," said Sam. "It's a piece of cake."

On the long drive back to her house, Sam found she could not sit with a quiet mind while the goat chewed

on her clothes. Remembering how quickly the philodendron had disappeared, she was afraid she might
end up as bare as Lady Godiva. "Stop that," she kept
exclaiming, wiggling to get out of his reach. She
pushed him away from her shirt with her hands, but
he only butted at her with his head and began tugging
at the waist of her jeans. "Stop it," she said. "Luke!
He's eating my hair."

At last, Luke pulled his car into Sam's driveway
behind the family cars. To Sam's relief, no barking
announced their return. Fruity seemed to have gone
back to sleep.

Luke opened the trunk and got out the bale of hay.
Sam could hear the goat's soft baa inside the car. She
fingered her hair uneasily, hoping the goat had not
eaten a noticeable amount of it. "You two get the kitty
litter," Luke said. He lifted the bale of hay and began
staggering with it around to the back of the garage.

Once they were in the garage, they turned on the
light over her father's workbench and went to work
spreading out a layer of kitty litter on the section of
floor Sam had cleared for the goat. Then they spread
a generous amount of hay over the kitty litter and
Luke went to fetch the goat.

"I'd keep him tethered," Luke advised when he returned leading the goat. "You don't want him climbing all over the garage and eating the paint off your
car. Just keep him over in this one corner."

"Right," said Sam, snapping the tether on to the
goat's collar. She only hoped that the goat was willing to go along with their plan.

"You've already got the water dish set up," said Luke approvingly. "Good. Okay. We're all set. You two go on inside and get a good night's sleep. I'll see you Monday." He gazed at the bare light bulb over the workbench. "Monday we turn in our scoop," he said. "How do you think we ought to put it? Reliable sources tell us? No, maybe 'usually reliable sources.' Yeah, I like that."

The goat lay down on the hay, stretched to take a mouthful of hay and began to chew peacefully.

"No wonder he's fat," Sam commented. "He's always eating."

Luke opened the back door to the garage and gave a quick look around. From inside the house, Fruity gave the alarm with full-throated baying.

"Fruity's a good watchdog," Luke observed.

"Oh, get out of here," said Sam, exasperated by his calm. "Come on, Marcy. We'd better move." The beagle's cry seemed to bounce off the neighbors' houses, its volume magnified.

The two girls hurried around the house to Sam's front door and Sam opened the door slowly. She thought she would never get used to how spooky her own house could seem at night—the shadows, the odd squares of pale light and the sound of the beagle baying in the pantry. The two girls tiptoed in, locked the door behind them and began cautiously making their way up the stairs in the darkness. Too late, Sam remembered that the third stair had a creak in it. When Marcy stepped on it, the noise was so loud that she lost

her nerve and Sam had to give her a little push to keep
her moving.

The two girls had just reached Sam's bedroom at
the top of the stairs, when Sam heard her father's
bedroom door open. "Get in the bed," Sam said ur-
gently. "Hurry."

Wide-eyed, Marcy leaped into the bed, shoes and
all. The springs groaned as Sam jumped in the bed
after her. They swiftly pulled the coverlet up to their
chins. Sure enough, a moment later the door to Sam's
bedroom opened slowly and her father stuck his head
in. Sam closed her eyes and tried to breathe heavily.
She wondered if she dared try faking a snore. To her
relief, the door soon closed. Sam heard the third stair
creaking as her father made his way downstairs.

Fruity, who had been baying more or less
constantly, finally quieted and Sam heard her father
come upstairs muttering.

She and Marcy lay frozen for some minutes after his
footsteps passed their door, afraid to move. Sam
stared wide-eyed at the faint strips of light cast on the
coverlet by the venetian blind. Finally Marcy whispered, "I'm not cut out for this kind of thing. I'm
quivering all over like Jell-O."

"A miss is as good as a mile," whispered Sam, who
was feeling badly shaken herself. "But golly, that was
close!" She didn't even like to think of what would
have happened if her father had looked in the room
and found the bed empty. No explanation in the world
could have covered for their being missing at 1 a.m.

"Sam, I really appreciate your helping Luke out with this," Marcy whispered. "I know you didn't want to do this."

"Oh, well, I wouldn't want to miss out," said Sam. "This may be my last chance to participate in his criminal activities."

"He wants a big story so much," said Marcy. "It's important to him. I know it seems dumb to us, but I want to do everything I can to make this last year really great for him."

"I wish you wouldn't put it that way. It makes it sound like we're all going to die instead of just graduate."

"We have to face it, Sam. We're going in different directions. You and I might end up at the same college, but I'm not even sure Luke is going to college at all. How could he with his grades? He's talking about trying to get a job on the *Banner* after graduation, writing obituaries. After this year, we're going to be living in different worlds."

"Not so different," said Sam. "If we go to Carolina, we can still come home pretty often. We can all get together on the weekends."

Sam could feel the bed jiggling a little and she realized Marcy was vigorously shaking her head. "Sam, listen," said Marcy. "I have a list."

That did not surprise Sam. Marcy liked lists almost as much as Sam did, but hers were always more logical and achievement oriented. You'd never catch Marcy with a note on her list about checking out voodoo.

"Okay, you have a list," repeated Sam. Why was she so sure she didn't want to hear this?

"It's this list of the top colleges in the country. It starts up at the top with Stanford, Harvard, Yale and Princeton, then the University of California at Berkeley."

"You know this list by heart?"

"Just about. Then come Dartmouth and Duke and places like the University of Chicago and the University of Michigan and Brown, then comes the University of North Carolina at Chapel Hill. I'm going to whatever school is highest on the list as long as it gives me the financial aid I need."

"You wouldn't go to school in California!" protested Sam. "It's so far away. And everybody's strange out there. They have cults. They eat goat cheese and avocados and strange stuff like that."

"Sure, I would go to California. I want to go to the highest ranking school I can, wherever it is."

Sam was sure there was a flaw in Marcy's thinking. "But you haven't even talked about any small schools. Most of the ones you've mentioned are these huge schools that everybody knows about. There are a lot of small schools where you get just as good an education, maybe better."

"I don't want a good education. You can get a good education at the library. I want a famous school. I'm not going to make the mistake my mother did," said Marcy. "She followed her heart all the way and look what it got her. A garage apartment with all the paint peeling. She actually majored in music. Music! Could anything be worse? This is a lady who actually fell in love with a musician and imagined they'd be playing duets their whole life. Talk about naive. Not for me. I want to be able to call up some company and say 'I was Phi Beta Kappa at such and such big famous school.' And they'll say, 'Yes, ma'am. Come right in and here's your key to the executive washroom.'"

"I have a feeling it might not work exactly like that," said Sam.

"Close enough," said Marcy.

Sam was thinking how parallel her own case was. Her grades were good, but obviously not in a class with Pip's. Did that mean that she and Pip, too, were "going in different directions"?

"So where does Luke fit into all this?" asked Sam, sure she would not like the answer.

"He doesn't," said Marcy. There was an uncertain quaver in her voice. "Unless I do end up at Carolina, we'll just have this one year and then it's pfft."

"Pfft?"

"Over. That's why I wanted to do this goat thing for him."

"But I thought you were crazy about Luke?"

"I can't let that matter. Don't you see?"

It gave Sam the creeps to hear Marcy talk about cutting Luke out as if she were going at her life with a huge pair of shears. What did she do about her feelings for him? Wasn't cutting Luke out going to be like cutting herself?

Sam kicked off her shoes and wiggled her bare toes under the covers. "Maybe you'll find somebody you like better when you're off at college."

"No, I won't," Marcy whimpered. "But that's just the way it's got to be."

Sam wondered what Pip would think of Marcy's plans. She knew she couldn't ask him. That question would cut too close to her own heart. It took her a long time to get to sleep.

Chapter Four

Sunday night, Sam's father, in a flour-spattered apron, was standing at the stove serving himself a second helping of chili. "I see you've already taken the garbage out," he said. "That's good."

"While Mom is away we need to pull together," Sam said virtuously. Actually she had no choice but to take out the garbage. She couldn't risk her Dad's going out to the garbage cans where he might notice the telltale discarded hay, kitty litter and goat smells.

"I hope we're not going to get tired of chili before your mother gets back. It seems to be the only thing I know how to fix."

They were eating at the kitchen table and weren't bothering much about such niceties as serving dishes and tablecloths. The number of dirty dishes to be washed had dropped precipitously since Sam's mother had left. Sam's mother went in for things like poached pears with raspberry sauce, which required two pots, a blender and a serving dish. Sam and her dad favored simple and classic items like corn chips, which could be eaten right out of the bag at a tremendous saving of time and energy. The taste was not exactly the same, of course.

Her father sat down at the kitchen table and yawned. "I'm going to turn in early tonight," he said. "I hardly slept at all last night with the way Fruity was carrying on. Did you hear that racket?"

"He was barking some, wasn't he?"

"Barking? It sounded like the last trumpet. He's always jumpy like that when your mother is away. It was the same way when she went to that child abuse conference last spring."

"I guess that's it," Sam agreed. "He senses that something is different and it makes him nervous so he just barks at the slightest little noise." She jumped up from the kitchen table. "Maybe I'll just empty all the wastebaskets now, too."

"You don't have to get carried away with the garbage detail, you know. The trash can wait."

"I like to stay on top of it," she said.

While her father's back was turned, she took a few carrots out of the crisper and dropped them in the kitchen wastebasket. Then she collected another wastebasket from the living room and headed out back. It was dark and she had to pick her way carefully back to the garbage cans to keep from tripping over the hoses that were carelessly coiled near the garden.

First she emptied the wastebaskets, then took a quick look around her and darted into the garage. She was glad her family's house was the old, inconvenient kind with the garage at the back of the lot. That made it all the less likely that her father would hear the goat.

Grogan was chewing meditatively on his rope when Sam looked in on him. She put the carrots in his food dish, then scratched his head just behind the ears. He responded to this attention by bending down to chew delicately on her shoe.

"What's wrong with your regular food, huh? You don't seem to like that goat food from the feed store," said Sam, stepping away from him. "Let me guess. You like the thrill of the forbidden, right? Like Luke."

By the time she got back to the kitchen, her father was dropping his empty chili bowl into soapy water. "You took your time," he commented. "I was starting to come looking for you."

"I just stood out there for a while thinking and, uh, looking at the stars."

"Out by the garbage cans you were thinking? You're not in love or anything are you, Sam?"

She flushed.

Her father seemed to regret teasing her because he turned back to washing the dishes. "Maybe I ought to go out and look at the stars myself. We might as well enjoy this good weather while we've got it," he said. "It won't last much longer."

Sam realized that he was trying to give her a little personal space and she was grateful to him. But at the same time it made her feel like the lowest kind of sneak for pulling something over on him.

The next day at newspaper staff, Luke produced his news story, all typed and ready to go. "Nashua Mascot Disappears."

"Wow! Somebody's really got their goat!" snickered Reggie. "Who did it? Hey, wait a minute, Luke. Your source didn't happen to be one of the kidnappers, did it?"

"It was an anonymous tip," said Luke. "But I checked on the story by phoning a couple of members of the Nashua football team and they confirmed it. They found out the goat was missing when one of their guys went by Sunday to feed him."

"Do they have any clues to who did it?"

"I don't know. I had to hang up all of a sudden. Those guys started acting like I might have something to do with it."

"What's this?" asked Mr. Perkins, looking up from the papers he was marking.

"We've got a real news story, Mr. Perkins," said Luke. "The Nashua mascot has been kidnapped."

"I'm not sure we should print that," said Mr. Perkins. "We don't want to stir up bad feelings between the two schools so close to the game."

"But it's our first real news story!" Luke burst out. "This is no time for censorship. What ever happened to freedom of the press?"

"It'll be all over school pretty soon anyway, Mr. Perkins," Marcy said. "We might as well write it up." She looked down at her hands. "Even if we don't print a word, the kidnappers will be spreading the story all over school anyway. What would be the point of kidnapping Nashua's mascot unless you made sure everybody knew about it?"

"I must admit there is some truth in what you say, Marcy." Mr. Perkins frowned. "All right, Luke. You have my permission. Go ahead with the story."

Luke breathed a sigh of relief.

"Naturally, we will print an editorial at the same time deploring this development," added Mr. Perkins. "Luke can write that."

Luke's face reflected mixed emotions, but Sam could see that on the whole the humor of the situation appealed to him. He was not the sort to fret about the fine shades of ethical questions.

Happy was regarding Luke thoughtfully. "I happen to know a guy who's on the Nashua team," she said.

"That figures," said Anita sourly.

"I think I can find out whether or not they have any lead on who did it," Happy said. "Who is going to get the byline on this story?"

"It can be two stories," Luke said. "I'll do a story on the rivalry between the two schools, which culminated in this outrageous and dastardly act, and you can do a story on the investigation from the Nashua point of view, if you can get enough material."

"I'll get enough," said Happy. She was regarding her perfectly manicured thumb. "Don't you worry about that."

Sam, for one, didn't doubt it. Happy might be short on human warmth but she was long on determination.

The *Traveler* wasn't due to come out until Friday, and it would, of course, have been better if everyone on newspaper staff could have kept the goat story quiet until then, but the staffers naturally assumed that, as Marcy had suggested, the kidnappers would be spreading the news themselves so they saw no need to keep quiet. As a consequence, by the end of the day most of the school had at least heard rumors that the Nashua mascot was missing.

A poster depicting a black goat had already appeared mysteriously by the door to the cafeteria with the legend, "Have you seen this kid?"

Pip met Sam in the parking lot after school as usual. "Let's go by Baskin-Robbins, okay?" He touched her cheek gently with his finger.

Sam beamed at him. "Oh, great," she said. "Tell you what. Why don't you follow me home and we can go to Baskin-Robbins in your car?"

Excitement was spreading through the school about the kidnapping of Nashua's mascot and Sam was secretly beginning to feel a little like a heroine. Keeping quiet about her part in the heist was a bit of a strain and she was looking forward to showing Grogan to Pip and telling him, in strictest confidence, all about her adventure. Though she was sure he would have advised her against getting involved if he had been asked, she thought he might be able to see the funny side of it now that it was over and done with. And Grogan really was cute. She thought Pip might like him.

When they got to Sam's house, she jumped out of her car. "I have to run inside a minute. Meet me behind the garage," she called. "I want to show you something." Pip stuck his head out the open window of his car. "Is this some kind of surprise or something?"

"I guess you could say that." She ran up the front steps, hurried into the kitchen and got several carrots out of the fridge. She knew Grogan would not make a good first impression on Pip if he started out by nibbling on his shirt. She also took the precaution of taking a soup bone out of the freezer and tossing it to Fruity, who was stretched out in a spot of sun beneath the kitchen window. She hoped that would guarantee at least a little peace and quiet.

Pip was waiting for her behind the garage. "What's in there?" he asked. "I've been hearing funny sounds. Is it a sheep?"

Sam threw the door open with a single dramatic gesture. "See for yourself."

Pip peered into the musty interior of the garage. "Old bicycles?"

"No," said Sam. "Over there. Look over there in the corner!"

"Jee-rusalem," said Pip. "It's the goat."

"Grogan is his name," said Sam. She dropped the carrots into the goat's food dish. "It's a sweet little thing, isn't it?" Grogan leapt up lightly from his bed of hay and began examining the carrots. Sam had left the door cracked open and a beam of sunlight fell through the dusty air onto the hay.

"*You* were the one who kidnapped him, Sam?"

"Not single-handedly. I did have help."

"Don't tell me. Let me guess. This was one of Luke's bright ideas."

"Marcy was anxious to do it, too," said Sam. "She wanted Luke to have one big news story before he graduates." She hesitated a minute. "I wasn't exactly keen on it at first, but I have to admit it's gone pretty well so far. Nobody has the slightest suspicion who did it."

"I thought you were finished with Luke's schemes.. Why did you have to get involved?"

"They really needed me because neither of them has a garage where they could keep the goat. And the truth is I wanted to do it because this may be one of the last things we're in on together." Sam could feel a lump growing in her throat at the thought and she began to talk quickly. "I don't think we'll get caught. It's not obvious who could have taken it because the whole school had a motive. You know how worked up everybody is about that game. Doing it was really scary, though. Marcy and I had to sneak out of the house in the middle of the night and we almost got caught! We got back in the bed about a millisecond before Dad peeked in my room. I've already told Luke he can take Grogan back all by himself. I can't take another night like that. You aren't actually mad at me about getting mixed up in it, are you?"

"Heck, Sam, I think it's stupid, but I can never be mad at you," he said, putting his arms around her. "You're too important to me."

They kissed until Sam felt warm all over. Even her toes. She noticed the dust motes in the shaft of light seemed still, as if the tiny particles were in another dimension out of time. She could almost feel she was frozen in time herself. The moment was so perfect she wished it would last forever.

He pulled her down on the hay and she could feel his warm hands at her bare waist where her shirt was coming untucked. He was struggling with the buttons on her shirt and when it came open Sam felt a cold draft on the soft skin above her bra. She felt a rush of excitement at the quiet intimacy as his hand began slipping into her bra.

Suddenly she felt something tugging at her hair. She giggled and she saw a hurt look flash onto Pip's face. "It's Grogan!" she gasped. "He's eating my hair."

"Good Lord," said Pip, rolling away from her. Attracted by Pip's movement, Grogan tiptoed over on delicate hooves to take a bite of Pip's hair, too. Pip was fending him off with his hands. "What do you do with this goat, Sam?"

Sam got up and pulled Pip up off the hay. "You've got to get out of his way," she said. "Come over here where he can't reach you. He eats everything in sight. It's sort of his personality."

"Some personality." said Pip. He was dusting off his pants with his hands.

Sam pulled a straw out of her hair, buttoned up her blouse, and dusted off her skirt as well as she could.

"It's always something," said Pip. "We never get any time by ourselves. Not any real time."

Sam put her arms around his neck and kissed his lips lightly. "I guess I'd better go in and brush this hay out of my hair before my father gets home," she said.

"That's just what I mean," said Pip. "If it's not one thing it's something else. Look, Sam, we love each other, right?"

She answered him with another kiss. She could have kissed him for hours, but he held her tightly and began to speak.

"So why don't we go away together for the weekend, huh?"

She blinked. "We couldn't do that."

"Sure, we could."

"What would our parents say?"

"Do you tell your parents everything? I've been talking about driving over to the library at State to do some research for my senior thesis. I can just say I'm going to drive into Raleigh and stay for the weekend. You can say you're going somewhere with Marcy."

"I couldn't do that."

Pip let go of her. "I get it," he said bitterly. "You can sneak out of the house in the middle of the night to do something illegal with Luke, but you don't trust me enough to go to Raleigh with me."

"It's different," Sam said.

"You don't want to?"

"I don't feel right about it." Sam remembered her mother saying that there were some things, like marriage, that you didn't need a good excuse not to do. Not wanting to was reason enough. Suddenly she knew that sex was one of those things. She didn't feel right about going away with Pip. She wasn't ready for that.

"All right, Sam, it's okay. You're never going to catch me pushing you into anything." He was turning away from her. "I'm not like Luke. But I don't know how much of this I can take. Maybe we're just seeing too much of each other, maybe that's it. We're making out at the movies, making out in parking lots, making out in garages. It's driving me crazy."

"We could stop making out," she suggested tentatively.

He did not smile. "We could start seeing other people," he said.

Sam hurt so much she was not sure she could swallow. She finally managed to whisper, "Yes, we could do that." She felt humiliated that she could not make her voice sound normal when Pip was standing there looking at her so calmly.

"Do you understand that I just can't take it anymore, Sam? I don't know what else to do."

"Whatever you think," she said. "It's fine. Really."

After he had gone, she stood there for some time watching the motes of dust hovering in the beam of light.

Chapter Five

"What do you mean you and Pip are seeing other people!" Marcy shrieked.

Sam was lying on her stomach on Marcy's bed. She thought about it a moment and then corrected herself. "I mean Pip will probably start seeing other people," she said. "I on the other hand will probably waste away until I am nothing but a shadow of my former self."

Marcy sat down on the bed suddenly. "You will do no such thing," she said. "Nobody wastes away anymore. That went out at the turn of the century. What happened between you and Pip? I thought you two were gaga about each other?"

"I am still gaga. Pip is only ga."

"You don't have to be flip with me, Sam. I'm your best friend. What did that creep do to you?"

"Nothing. It's only that for the greater development of our personalities and interests we have both decided it would be wiser not to tie ourselves down to just one person."

"Is that what he told you? What a line!"

Sam, who had made it all up herself and thought rather well of it, tried not to look hurt. "I am having a little difficulty adjusting to being a free agent, but I am sure I will look back on this one day soon as a wonderful opportunity for growth and change."

"You hate growth and change, Sam. You still have your first teddy bear."

A tear welled up in Sam's eye at the thought of her faithful teddy bear, the one warm and loving constant in her life. Tears seemed to be welling up in her eyes a good bit since yesterday afternoon.

"Marcy, can I ask you a very personal question?"

"Sure, Sam. I don't have any secrets from you."

"Are you and Luke sleeping together?"

"Aha!" said Marcy, jumping up. "So that's what it was. That creep was pressuring you to have sex with him, wasn't he? I just knew it—out for what he can get, spoiled, a rich kid used to having his own way. I knew he was that kind of boy."

Sam was accustomed to the way Marcy and Luke were always criticizing Pip and she refused to get upset about it at this point when she had bigger worries. "You didn't answer my question."

"What?"

"Are you and Luke sleeping together?"

"Oh. No. We aren't."

"You wouldn't lie to me about this, would you, Marce?"

"I might," said Marcy candidly. "But I'm not."

"You're not?"

"No. I've already told you, Sam, that I don't see any future with Luke, and with my luck, we could be using three kinds of birth control and I'd get pregnant anyway. That would fix things. So much for my going to a really good school then. So we don't."

"Very sensible. Very reasonable. Very like you, Marcy."

"Also," said Marcy. "I'm afraid if we started sleeping together, I really might not be able to give him up. It's bad enough already. What if I got so totally hooked on him that I was willing to let my future go smash?"

Sam leaned on her elbow. It was nice to be looking at other peoples' problems for a change.

"So how does Luke feel about that?" she asked in a detached voice.

"Well, of course, I haven't told him about the no future part. But we've talked some about this sex thing and he respects my decision. Maybe he's not sure he wants to get as committed as that, either. Do you think that can be what's going on?"

Sam rolled back on her stomach. "I don't think at all. My mind is completely numb. My last rational thought was at about 3:30 yesterday afternoon."

Marcy looked at her sympathetically. "Sam, he's not worth it."

"That's what you think," said Sam thickly.

Sam's father was out at a meeting of the library board, and when she got back to the house the phone was ringing unanswered. Sam groped clumsily for the key, then ran into the house, knocking over a dining-room chair in her progress to the kitchen. To her hypersensitive ears the phone sounded as if it had been ringing a long time. She was sure it was Pip.

She grabbed at it. "Hello?"

"Sam?"

"Oh, hi, Luke," she said in a flat voice.

"Is something wrong?"

"Nope, everything's hunky-dory. I am merely facing a few difficult adjustments in my personal quest for maturity."

"That's good. Look, Sam, I've been thinking about the goat."

"You promised me you were going to take Grogan back by yourself," she reminded him.

"I know, I know. That's not what I'm talking about. I've been thinking about it, see, and if we return Grogan before the *Traveler* even comes out, the story loses a lot of its punch. Do you see that?"

"I guess so," said Sam. "What's another couple of days, anyway. I'll keep him until Friday."

"I knew you'd see that, Sam. But here's an angle you might not have thought about, and let me just say before I go on that I'm bringing you out a new bale of hay tomorrow, right after school. It's already in the trunk of my car.''

"What is the angle, Luke?'' She was not even particularly curious. She had a strange passive feeling as if it were her fate to simply stand at the telephone, immobile, while disaster after disaster washed over her.

"Only that it's just hit me that we could build this into another story if we handle it right. The question is, will the loss of their mascot affect the Nashua team's performance? I thought I might try some telephone interviews with local psychologists, ask them about morale and psyching people out, the effects of superstition on athletes' performance, that kind of thing. It's a juicy topic. Lots to it.''

"But then we'd have to keep the goat until after the Nashua-Lee game!''

"That's right. Neat idea, isn't it? After all, the tough part is snatching the goat. Just by keeping it an extra week we get more of the good out of the kidnapping. More miles per gallon of risk, you might say.''

If Sam had had her normal strength she would have pointed out that the only reason keeping the goat seemed less risky to him was that risk fell solely on her. But it didn't seem worth pointing out. What were a couple of weeks when her life seemed to stretch endlessly empty ahead of her? She even discerned in herself a faint unwillingness to part with Grogan. He was a nice goat. He seemed to like her. And he was the only witness to everything coming apart between her and Pip. Maybe she would talk it over with him sometime. He might be able to shed a little light on it. More than she could anyway.

"Are you still there, Sam?"

"Yes."

"So what do you think? Isn't that a great idea?"

"Okay."

"What did you say?" asked Luke, his voice rising in elation. "I mean, thanks. I knew you'd see it that way, Sam. Thanks a lot. I won't forget this, believe me."

Pip could not remember ever feeling such black despair. Sam had stood in that dusty old garage and watched him walk out of her life without raising a finger to stop him. He could hardly believe it.

But maybe she had been cooling on him for some time. She had laughed at him. No, that was because of the goat. The blasted goat had been nibbling on her hair. He had to keep reminding himself of that. The fact was he wasn't thinking too clearly. He had both the vague feeling that he had been somehow at fault and the simultaneous conviction that he had suffered from some monstrous injustice.

Did she have to look at him as if he were a criminal when he had suggested they go away for the weekend? People were at it all over town, in the back seats of cars, behind park bushes, in vans at rock concerts—and these were people who hardly knew each other, people with infectious diseases, even. All he did was talk about a quiet weekend together with the girl he loved and she acts like he's Jack the Ripper. He was living his life all wrong, that was for sure.

Maybe he would go back to her and—the heck he would. Sam had shown him what she thought of him and he wasn't going to give her the satisfaction of seeing him come crawling back. The only thing was that he was hurting so bad he was going to have to watch it or it was going to start affecting his grades. He'd seen it happen to a lot of people.

He laid his calculus book on his desk and opened it. The page seemed to swim before his eyes and he saw Sam's face instead. How could she not trust him after all the time they'd gone together? How could she imagine that he would ever hurt her?

This was the sort of thing he needed to hash out with somebody who was more objective. Not his father, who was from another generation and who had practically invented the term straight laced. Or, he shuddered, his mother, who had been brought up in Spain and as near as he could make out had never gone anyplace without a chaperone until she came to this country. What he needed was a best friend. The problem was that Sam was his best friend. He groaned.

With his mind flying continually from calculus to Sam, it seemed like hours before he was able to push the book aside and an eternity before he was able to get any sleep.

The next morning when Pip got to school, his head was aching. He decided to talk to the first person he met. It was the only way he could keep himself from continually combing the crowd with hurt eyes, looking for Sam.

"Hiya, Happy," he said. He leaned against the brick wall.

"Hi," said Happy. She had a way of opening her eyes wide when she saw him. "Have you heard about how we've stolen Nashua's mascot?" she asked.

He was startled. He was sure Sam hadn't mentioned Happy being in on the heist. "*You* stole him?"

"Not me personally," she said. "I meant the kids from our school. I would never have the nerve to do something like that."

She touched his sweater. "You've got something on you," she murmured. He looked down and saw that she was plucking off a silvery hair that glittered in the sunlight. Sam's hair. Happy dropped the hair with a smile and gently brushed his sweater with her fingertips.

Pip remembered hearing guys say that Happy was sexy and now he could see what they meant. It was the way she touched you. She hadn't done anything that couldn't be construed in the most innocent way and yet he had the growing conviction that she was coming on to him. You didn't go around touching guys unless you had some kind of hidden agenda. Just recognizing that restored his battered self-confidence and he found himself smiling at her.

"You going anyplace after school?" he asked.

Her hand hesitated in midair. She was surprised, all right, he realized. But that was because everybody still thought he was going with Sam.

"Nowhere in particular," she said, looking up at him worshipfully.

It was funny in a way. She laid it on so thick. But at least he felt he knew where he was with her. He could feel himself expanding under her gaze.

"We might go by and get a bite to eat," he suggested. "Pizza, maybe."

"I just *love* pizza," she said, never taking her eyes off of his. "I like it with *everything* on it. I guess I've always been greedy." Her tongue flicked out and licked the corner of her mouth and Pip could feel himself getting breathless. There was nothing subtle about this girl, but the odd thing was that even as he was finding the come-on mildly comical, he was beginning to feel there might be some fun left in his life after all.

"Meet you at Fino's after school?" he suggested.

"I'll be there," she said.

The bell rang and Pip turned away.

Sam saw him walking to homeroom with a faint smile on his lips and felt as if her heart were being sliced in two.

Happy fled to the bathroom to regain her composure. She didn't care whether or not she was late to class. She leaned against the cool tile of the wall and counted backward from twenty to calm herself.

She had planned this moment for a long time. She had waited, plotted, attended incredibly boring science club meetings, hung out at that same spot by the administration building day after tedious day. All that time she had never doubted that at last she would succeed in attracting Pip, but she had expected more of a struggle. It was the suddenness of his giving in that had thrown her off balance. She stared at the pale oval of her face in the cracked mirror over the basin—perfect hair, perfect makeup, carefully plucked brows. She knew she was attractive, but Sam was no slouch in the looks department, either, and she and Pip Byron had been practically glued together ever since he had come to town.

"Thank you, God. Thank you, thank you, thank you," she murmured, raising her hands to readjust her earrings. At last she was going to be able to get back at Sam Morrison. How she was going to love watching Sam fall apart the way she herself had crumbled at that embarrassing, never-to-be-forgotten dance last year when Jim Shipman had dropped her.

And going out with the Byron boy might be fun, too. As far as looks went he was nothing special, and he was too dark for her taste, too, almost foreign looking. But he was the richest boy in town and he had a super car. She smiled at the delightful thought of riding around town in Pip's Mercedes convertible. In a short while, she promised herself, Pip Byron was going to have a hard time wondering how he had lived without her.

That afternoon after school, Pip's one thought was that he didn't want to run into Sam in the parking lot. He didn't know what he would do if he saw her. He might even wreck his car, he was that upset. So he sort of hung around the gym some and ran a few laps with the guys there. It felt good to be doing something physical, to be working up a sweat. Coach Jamison flagged him down. "Going out for tennis team, Byron?"

"Maybe," said Pip, who hadn't considered it.

"We could use you," said the coach. "Think about it."

Pip fell in with a few guys doing pull-ups and ended up right next to Reggie Baker, a guy who was in his physics class. Sweat was beading on Reggie's forehead, but he sketched a nod in Pip's direction as he continued pulling up. Pip remembered Sam saying that Reggie knew everybody.

"What do you know about Happy Chambers, Reg?" Pip asked suddenly.

"Shark-infested waters," said Reg.

"What did you say?" asked Pip, sure he had heard wrong.

Reggie wiped his brow with a towel and stood looking at Pip with a faintly mystified expression. "What you want to know about her for? Thought you were with Sam?"

"Just curious," said Pip.

"Curiosity killed the cat, man." Reggie grinned. He jogged a little in place and then took off jogging around the gym.

"Aw, heck," muttered Pip. He had just remembered that he had a date with Happy right now, at this very minute. He had been concentrating so much on not running into Sam that he had forgotten all about meeting Happy. He bolted for the showers.

When he got to Fino's he squinted anxiously at the darkened restaurant, wondering if she had already left. Then he spotted her. She was drumming her fingers on a table. He saw her look at her watch. Unaccountably he was reminded of the night he had seen her slap Sam. Her face was pale against her artfully tousled hair and her mouth looked set.

"Sorry I'm late," he said, as he slid into the booth. "I got held up."

She smiled at him. "Oh, are you late? I didn't notice. I just got here myself."

"Maybe I'd better go up and put in our order. Are you hungry?"

"Well, I am but I have to constantly watch my weight."

As she touched her hand to her waistline Pip found his eyes inexorably following her hand down and he had to jerk them back to her face with an effort of will. "Everything on it, you say?" he stuttered.

"Everything," she smiled. She had some sort of brown shadow above her lids and something on her eyelashes, too. He supposed if she got caught in the rain, muddy brown rivulets would run down her face, but he had to admit that the effect was striking.

He jumped up to order the pizza, glad to get away from her for a moment. While he stood at the counter waiting his turn, he puzzled over the way Happy's every word and gesture seemed halfway suggestive. What kind of person could she be? High-strung, he supposed, remembering the scene at the dance. This was not a girl who was easy to read. Lots of hidden stuff going on there. Maybe that was what Reggie had meant by "shark-infested waters." He recalled that there had been something hard in her look when he had just come in. She gave you the feeling you weren't quite sure what she would do next. One thing was certain—she couldn't have been more different from Sam, and that was good because the one thing he needed above all was to get his mind off Sam.

He glanced around the restaurant wondering if there was any chance Sam would come in. "May I take your order?" asked the freckle-faced kid behind the counter.

"Small pizza, crispy crust, everything on it," said Pip.

"Your number will be fifteen," said the boy.

Pip pocketed the slip of paper the boy gave him, then stared at the door as if by looking at it he could will Sam to come in. He had the half-formed plan of making her jealous, though it was not very clear to him what he hoped to accomplish that way. He supposed she was off somewhere with Luke and Marcy, as usual. Those two would be euphoric when they found out he and Sam had split. Thinking of that, he was so lost in a momentary feeling of black hatred toward Luke and Marcy that on his way back to the booth he almost ran into the salad bar. He sat down across from Happy frowning.

"So, where are you from? Originally, I mean," asked Happy.

"Alexandria. Near D.C."

"Do you like it here?"

Pip's face darkened as he thought of Sam, who had made the move to this awful little town tolerable, who had loved him before she even knew that he was Pip Byron, heir to the Byron tobacco fortune. He remembered the first time he had seen her, a long-legged girl clambering out of a dusty car at Westridge Plaza. She had been wearing short shorts with an old man's felt hat pulled down almost to her ears and had been a sight that was at once comical and unutterably lovely. Until then, he had never really believed in love at first sight.

"A lot of people think Fenterville is too small," Happy volunteered when he didn't speak. "Honestly, if I can ever get away from here I'm never coming back. There's no culture here, no arts, nothing. This place is literally nowhere. I mean, unless you're into tobacco warehouses, what does it have to offer? Zero."

"You're on the newspaper staff at school, aren't you?" asked Pip abruptly.

"I run it," said Happy, examining her thumbnail.

"I thought Luke was the editor."

"Technically. But I'm the assistant editor and a lot of the responsibility falls on me. If you knew Luke— well, maybe I'd better stop right there. I don't want to say anything ugly." She smiled and rubbed her bare foot against his leg.

"Number fifteen," called a nasal voice from the counter.

"Is that our order?" asked Happy.

"In a minute," said Pip. "So you've been on the staff right along, huh? I guess all you kids know each other."

"Oh, yes. But some of those kids are such *impossible* people." She rolled her eyes. "Frankly they need more *control* than Luke is willing to give. Luke should come down hard on them, make them toe the line. You can't have everybody going their own way on a newspaper. You've got to have order, discipline. You need a tight ship."

Pip noticed that Happy's critique of Luke's style as editor conflicted somewhat with her claim that she was in fact running the paper but he was too polite to point it out. "I'd better get that pizza," he said.

When he returned with it and put it down on the table, he realized that what he was really hungry for was not pizza but news of Sam. How did she look? Did she seem happy? This girl would know about that, but there was no way he could find it out without asking her outright and he didn't think that would be a good idea.

Happy lifted a triangle of pizza to her mouth and took a bite so carefully that not a bit of tomato sauce touched the corners of her mouth and not a strip of mozzarella escaped, but Pip was staring over her shoulder at the door and missed her startling performance.

"Aren't you going to have some before it gets cold?" Happy asked him, looking at him uneasily.

"I'm not really that hungry," he said. Maybe he would drive by Sam's house this evening, he thought.

It might be better to use his mother's car, since his own convertible was so easily recognizable. He would just drive by her house and—do what? Look at her house. Yes, that was it, in case he could see her.

He suddenly picked up a piece of pizza and bit savagely into it.

Happy watched him with widening eyes. This guy ate as if the pizza were his worst enemy. She had heard he was smart but it must be another one of those unfounded rumors. As far as she could tell he had no brains, and no conversation. She wondered what Sam saw in him.

"I guess you were hungrier than you thought," she said, looking at the pizza crust he had tossed into the box. "Of course, someone as tall as you are needs to eat a lot more than little girls like me." She batted her eyelashes at him.

He did not even smile. She had the feeling he wasn't really paying attention to her. She was going to have to take immediate steps or he would slip right out of her grasp. She cleared her throat. "You know the new Ribault Cinema?"

"The place that's opening up at the mall?"

"Yes. It's going to be very special, crystal chandeliers, plush seats, just like the old-fashioned movie houses. My father was given a couple of tickets to the opening night. Want to go?"

"Okay."

"I'll give you a call after I check the time," said Happy.

"All right."

She licked her lips in satisfaction. She had done it. They had a second date. Tonight she would call up everyone she knew and give them the news that she was seeing Pip Byron. She wanted to be sure Sam heard about it as soon as possible.

Outside on the sidewalk, Sam was walking between Luke and Marcy toward Fino's front door.

"Look, Sam," said Luke in a low voice, "this is important. Did you tell Pip about the goat heist?"

"She wouldn't do that," said Marcy indignantly. Then she saw the look on Sam's face and fell suddenly silent.

"Oh, she told him all right. That's what I was afraid of," said Luke. "How much does he know, Sam? Everything?"

Sam nodded. "But Pip would never tell on us," she whispered. "Never." Just then she saw three big boys in purple-and-orange letter sweaters approaching from the opposite direction. "Oh, my gosh," she muttered. "Don't look now, but it's some guys from Nashua. Let's turn around."

Luke gripped her elbow firmly and spoke through clenched teeth. "Don't be stupid, Sam. If we turn around that will only make them suspicious. You keep walking right into Fino's."

"I think they're coming to Fino's, too," said Marcy nervously.

"So?" said Luke. "Those guys from Nashua are all over the place. Where else are they going to go for pizza but into town? There's no pizza out there in the ploughed fields. Listen, we can't run every time we see a purple-and-orange letter sweater."

"Why not?" asked Sam.

"Hey, Deever!" yelled one of guys in the sweater. "Isn't that the girl that tried to steal Grogan?"

With Luke's hand in the small of her back pushing her, Sam continued to lurch toward the boys though every instinct told her to run. Finally they were less than ten feet from the Nashua boys.

"Hi," Sam said. She ventured to wiggle her fingers at them in a little half wave.

"Grogan's missing," Deever said to her, his brows lowered. "This time it's for real."

"I heard," said Sam. "I'm sorry about that. I hope you find him."

"Oh, we will," said a taller guy behind Deever. "And when we do—" He made an eloquent wringing gesture with his hands and Sam could feel herself beginning to tremble.

"Well, good luck," said Sam. She pushed open the door to Fino's and groped her way to the first booth. Her eyes had not yet adjusted to the relative darkness inside.

"You were great," said Luke in a low voice. He sat down and watched as the boys from Nashua followed them in and took a booth on the other side of the salad bar. "You almost had me convinced you were innocent, Sam."

"It wasn't too hard. I just pretended to myself that I didn't know anything about it. I have a very good imagination."

"Oh, my God,"˒ said Marcy. She laid her hand on top of Sam's.

Sam turned around, following Marcy's gaze, and saw that three booths behind her Pip was sitting with Happy. She was sure that all the blood in her head must be draining down to her shoes.

"Sam," whispered Marcy. "Do the way you were just doing a minute ago with those boys. Pretend it doesn't matter to you. Pretend you don't care."

Tears began streaming down Sam's cheeks. "I can't," she choked.

"God, Sam, can't you stop it?" said Luke. "Those guys over there are still looking at us. They're going to think you've got a guilty conscience or something."

"We've got to get out of here," said Marcy. "Sam can't take this."

"If we leave now those guys are going to follow us," warned Luke. "Pull yourself together, Sam."

Marcy rose a little out of her seat to get a better look at Pip. "I can't believe it," she whispered as she sat down. "Happy, of all people. How could he possibly pick her?"

"Because he's a blue-ribbon jerk, that's why," growled Luke.

Sam wiped her eyes with a paper napkin but the tears kept streaming down unabated. "I don't want to hear you say another word against Pip, Luke. We don't know for a fact that he has 'picked' her. For all we know they might have met here quite by accident." She blew her nose.

Marcy looked at her with pity. "We've got to get her out of here, Luke. This is cruel and unusual punishment."

"I just told you, Marce, we can't leave now."

"Honestly, Luke. Be reasonable."

"All right, but don't blame me if those goons come after us."

Sam was thankful that their booth was close to the door because when they rose to leave she discovered that her legs had become undependable. For a second or two she felt the same way she did when she had gotten out of bed after the flu, wobbly. She was glad when they were finally out of Fino's and she knew that even if she fell Pip would not see it happen. She actually felt sick.

Once they got to the car, she sat on the front seat between Luke and Marcy. Luke started up the car.

"So far, so good," Luke said, casting a look over his shoulder. "No sign of them."

"Is that all you can think about?" said Marcy. "Can't you see that Sam is in bad shape?"

"Good grief, Marce, every single one of them is bigger than me and there are three of them. Sure, I'm thinking of it. You think I want to end up as hamburger?"

Sam covered her eyes with her hand and sat silently between them.

After a moment, Luke patted her awkwardly on the back. "I'm sorry, Sam," he said.

"Don't," Sam said. She supposed she looked pretty pathetic. She didn't care.

Chapter Six

I can't stay," said Marcy, "because I've got to get to my job, but I just want to say one thing, Sam. You've got to get back in circulation."

Sam threw herself down on her bed. "You must be kidding."

"Pip's back in circulation, isn't he?"

"Please, Marcy. I just can't talk about that."

"I don't like to say this, Sam, because I know it sounds cruel, but you've got to face reality."

"The reality is that I am probably dying."

"Don't talk that way."

"Okay, who is going to ask me out? The word isn't out yet that Pip and I are—well, whatever we are. Nobody knows and I really think it's better that way until I can hear his name without wishing I were dead."

"We can set you up with a double date. Easy. I promise you it will cheer you up to get out."

"I feel sorry for the guy you pick for this date," said Sam. "I'll be crying all over him. Afterward he'll probably have to go home and wring out his shirt. 'That was some date I had with Sam Morrison,' he'll say. 'I nearly drowned.'"

"Honestly, Sam, you'll probably have fun. And believe me any number of guys are just dying to ask you out. Your face is pretty and has, if I may say so, winsome charm. Your legs are practically famous. And as far as disposition goes, you are sweet and kind."

Sam rolled over on her stomach and buried her face in her pillow. "You sound like a classified ad," she said in a muffled voice.

"I sound like your best friend," said Marcy. "Look, we'll get you on your feet again. Is it okay if I ask Luke to set something up?"

"Mmmph," said Sam.

"Good. I'm going to do that. Isn't your father usually home by now?"

Sam lifted her head. "He's at a special faculty meeting. I think it's about the goat."

"Golly, this is all too much to lay on you at once, Sam. I can see you're not up to coping with that goat anymore. Maybe I ought to get Luke to take him back tonight."

Sam shook her head. "I don't think so, Marcy. They'll be watching for us. I thought of it as soon as I saw those boys this afternoon. You saw their faces. Bent on revenge, that's what they were. I wouldn't be a bit surprised if they've booby-trapped the pen or set up an alarm or something. I think we'd better take Grogan to the stadium and let him go as soon as the game is over. That way we don't have to risk going back on the Nashua school grounds."

"I'm beginning to wish we had never gotten involved in taking that goat. Now it seems as if everything is happening at once."

Sam gave a crooked smile. "It's a part of the rich tapestry of life," she said.

"You wouldn't believe how much more human you look when you smile. Keep smiling. Now I've got to go. I'll see you tomorrow. Look, call me tonight if you're still feeling low, huh?"

A few minutes after Marcy left, Sam heard her father downstairs. She checked her face in the mirror and was relieved to see that there was no outward sign of the misery she felt.

"Sam!" called her father. "I'm home."

Sam went downstairs.

"Any letter from your mother?" he asked, leafing through the mail on the entry hall table.

"Nope."

"I think I'll call her tonight." He smiled ruefully. "I miss her."

You don't know what missing somebody is, Sam thought. Mom is only going to be gone two weeks total. Think of what it would be like if she might be gone for good. She took a deep breath. "So what was the meeting about?"

Her father frowned. "Mr. Hendley wants us to investigate this goat theft," he said. "He's appointed a special task force and I'm one of the lucky ones who get to serve on it."

"But you can't do anything!" she exclaimed, looking at him in alarm. "What does he expect?"

"I tried to tell him it was a job for the police. But he thinks the school is full of kids who know who's responsible and it's just a matter of getting one of them to talk. He imagines the teachers would be better at getting them to talk than the police would be. Maybe he's right. Sam, people keep telling me the newspaper is coming out with a story on the theft. Where are they getting their information from?"

"An anonymous tip," Sam said promptly. "Somebody called Luke."

"An anonymous tip, huh? Did Luke recognize the voice?"

"You'd have to ask him, Dad."

"I may do that. It's pretty embarrassing to our school, you know, to have our students do something like this, and if we don't catch these kids, some people are saying the thing may snowball. There could be retaliation from the Nashua kids, maybe real property damage. People could get hurt. Not that I can say I feel very hopeful about getting to the bottom of it."

"It sounds pretty hopeless, all right," said Sam, brightening. "I guess you didn't exactly want to be put on this special task force, huh?"

"You guess right. All committee work has its frustrating side but this is the worst."

Her father fixed chili dogs for supper. Chili was an amazingly versatile food. Sam foresaw endless possibilities—chili burgers, chili and tortilla chips, chili salad.

After supper, Sam could tell he was still thinking about the frustrations of working on faculty committees because he said, "You know, this might be a good time to fix that creaking stair. That's something that would give me a sense of accomplishment."

"I'll go get your tool chest," Sam said, getting up.

"You don't have to do that."

"It's my pleasure."

"I might not work on it just yet. Maybe I'll do it a little later."

"I'll go ahead and get the tool chest," said Sam. "Just in case you get the urge."

"You seem awfully anxious all of a sudden to go out and get the tool chest."

"That squeaky step has been driving me crazy," said Sam. Which was not entirely a lie. That step had given her some bad moments for sure.

Grogan was contentedly eating hay when she went out to the garage. Sam scratched him behind the ear and patted him on the rump. He nuzzled her pocket looking for carrots. "Well, Grogan," she said sadly

"Have you figured it out, yet? Is there any chance Pip will ever come back?"

How *could* Pip have asked Happy out? Was there any explanation besides the obvious one that Happy was sexy and he decided there was a good chance of getting her to go away with him for the weekend?

For a moment she toyed with the idea that Happy had pushed him out of the way of a speeding car or something. Common politeness would then have required Pip to say, "Since you have saved my life, perhaps you will let me treat you to a personal pan pizza."

Or possibly he had amnesia like those people on soap operas. A sudden blow on the head could have made him forget all he knew about Happy. And he would have forgotten about Sam, too.

As Sam walked back toward the house, carrying the heavy tool chest, she paused to wipe her eyes with her sleeve. The problem was that a much more plausible hypothesis sprang readily to mind, such as that Pip was strongly attracted to Happy. He wouldn't be the first.

When she got back in the house the phone was ringing.

"For you, Sam," said her Dad, holding the receiver out to her.

Sam took it from him, holding her breath. It had to be Pip. It just had to be. She would do anything, give up anything, if it would only be Pip. She would take out the garbage for an eternity and never complain.

"Hello," she croaked. She was glad that her father was drifting into the living room.

"Sam?" said Reggie's voice.

"Oh, hi, Reg."

"You don't sound like yourself."

"I may be coming down with a cold."

"Hey, after school today, Pip was asking me about Happy."

"What did you tell him?"

"Warned him, natch. But what can you say? Hey, are you and Pip still together or what?"

Sam licked her lips. "We're seeing other people," she said. This was a turning point, she realized. Since she had told Reggie, it would be all over school tomorrow. Well, what difference did it make, really, except that it meant she absolutely had to go out on that double date Marcy was so determined to set up. She would have to go unless she wanted everyone to go around saying that Pip had broken her heart.

"How about that. So you and Pip are seeing other people, huh?"

"It's a real opportunity for personal growth, as we see it."

"Sure. That's the way I see it, too."

"After all, this is our last year in high school. We owe it to ourselves to enjoy a variety of personal relationships."

"Sure thing. Well, I guess I better hit that trig."

"Me, too."

"Sam? Listen, I sure am sorry."

She had to hang up without saying goodbye because hearing the genuine sympathy in Reggie's voice, she could not trust herself to speak without bursting into tears.

She fixed herself a cup of tea and sat down at the kitchen table. It seemed to take her so long to do everything. She was slow to get the tea bag, slow getting down the cup and saucer. It was as if her batteries were running down. She stared at the phone, wishing it would ring.

Finally she picked up the paper and turned to the daily horoscope for counsel. A new month was beginning and she wondered if Aquarians were in for some better luck. Her eyes moving slowly down the column, she found her sign.

"Jupiter's conjunction with the moon on the 4th heralds a period designated to provide Aquarians with welcome opportunities. Many Aquarians have developed a keen culinary awareness in recent months. A rewarding occupation at this time might be to plant an herb garden."

Sam stared at the words with disbelief. An herb garden? Her life was in ruins and they were talking about planting an herb garden? She threw the paper down with disgust.

When she finished her tea, she trudged upstairs to her room and dialed Marcy's number. Marcy had said to call if she felt low. Well, she felt low all right. If she got any lower she would need CPR.

The line was busy. It figured. Her horoscope said plant an herb garden and her best friend's line was busy. That was life, right? If you had a lawn, you got crabgrass. If you had teeth, you got cavities. If you had love, you got heartbreak. She was surprised she hadn't noticed the symmetry and logic of it before.

Sam sat down at her desk and did her trig homework. She did not even care that she got half the answers wrong.

When she dialed Marcy's number later, she got through. "Who were you talking to?" she asked accusingly, as if she suspected Marcy of taking the phone off the hook on purpose to avoid her.

"Luke called. He's really worried that Pip is going to spill the story about the goat now that you two aren't going together. We talked a lot about whether there was some place we could move the goat to or whether we should try to return him."

"I guess Luke decided not to return him, but to hold tight and chance it."

"How did you know?"

"Oh, Marcy, Luke always decides to chance it. That's just the way he is. You've got to have noticed."

"Maybe he has taken a lot of risks in the past, but I can tell you this time he's pretty worried. I think he sees that this is something Mr. Perkins would never forgive him for. News manipulation you'd have to call it, wouldn't you? Of course, before it looked foolproof, almost. How could anybody find out with a whole school of suspects to choose from? But now there's this Pip angle. I have to admit it's got me worried. I keep asking myself what was he doing there with Happy. I mean, he's *got* to know she's your worst enemy. She clobbered you in front of hundreds of witnesses last year. Maybe the two of them are in cahoots now. Maybe they're plotting your downfall."

"If this is your idea of comfort, remind me not to call you again."

"Well, I've never done anything so risky as stealing that goat before. You think I'm getting a little paranoid?"

"Marcy, there's no reason for Pip to want to get back at me. Besides, he's not that kind of person."

"Well, what was he doing there with Happy?"

"I think that's pretty obvious," said Sam, swallowing. "He finds her attractive."

"Sam, she's got the personality of a tarantula. If he's thinking she's going to be as nice a person as you are he's in for a nasty shock."

"That's what I'm hoping. Tell me the truth, Marce. Do you think there's any chance he'll come back to me."

"Honestly, Sam, do you really want him back after all this?"

"I'd crawl to him on my hands and knees if I thought there was the tiniest chance."

"Maybe you'd even go away for the weekend with him?"

"Maybe I would."

"Sam! You are out of your flipping mind! You are nuts!"

Sam held the receiver away from her ear. "I am," she admitted. "I know it. I just can't seem to think straight."

"Oh, for pity's sake, give me strength. Where is your pride? Where is your common sense?"

"I don't know. Maybe I should work on those things."

"I'll say. Listen to yourself. You sound like the member of some harem. You are a free and independent woman. You don't have to take that kind of junk off a guy. If he can't appreciate the pleasure of your company then you can find someone who will."

"I miss him so much."

"I don't want to hear you talking in that crazy way anymore. Hang on to your self-respect. You're feeling low right now, but you'll feel much better later."

"You're right, Marcy. Maybe someday I'll look back on this and laugh. Ha, ha."

"Luke has already got something set up for Friday night. You know Bill Looney?"

"Yes, he's nice."

"Right, and he absolutely freaked out when Luke told him you were the girl he was getting matched up with. He idolizes you."

"That would be a nice change," admitted Sam wistfully. "But on the other hand, I am forced to point out that even if he does idolize me, it will probably not help that much. My horoscope takes a very pessimistic view of my life and so far it's been pretty much on target."

"Your horoscope?"

"Yes, Jupiter's conjunction with the moon, and then the transit of Mars through Libra."

"Sam, are you running a fever?"

"I could plant an herb garden," Sam went on with some bitterness. "I think I'd have a pretty good chance of success with an herb garden."

"Get hold of yourself! It sounds to me as if you're losing your grip on reality."

"Very possibly," said Sam sadly.

"I think I'll have Luke pick us both up at your house Friday night. Something tells me you may have trouble getting yourself in the right frame of mind for this date."

"You don't think an attitude like, say, 'tragic and resigned' will do?"

"No, I do not. You're going to have to do better. By the way, we're going to go to the opening of that fancy new theater."

"The one at the mall?"

"That's the one. And I promise you, you're going to have a perfectly wonderful time."

Chapter Seven

Marcy ran the brush through Sam's hair for the tenth time.

"You might as well give up. It always looks that way," said Sam. "Straight, blond, plain."

"I am not brushing your hair to make it look better," said Marcy grimly. "It looks fantastic. I am only trying to increase the blood circulation in your head."

"Forget it. I'm doomed."

Marcy threw up her hands. "I give up," she said. "What can I do when you have that attitude." She dropped the brush on the dressing table with a clatter and stomped out of the bedroom.

Sam leaned her chin on her hands and watched in the mirror as a tear trickled down her face. She was wearing out the patience of her friends. It was only a matter of time until she would be quite alone, forlorn. A hermit, no doubt.

A moment later, she heard Marcy's firm tread mounting the steps and the bedroom door flew open. "Your troubles are over, Sam," she said. She was waving the evening newspaper.

"Pip has murdered Happy?" suggested Sam, hopefully.

"Not quite that good, but listen to this. You're Aquarius, aren't you?"

"Yes, the watery sign," said Sam, wiping away another tear.

"Okay, now listen. Since Mars has completed its transit through Libra, Aquarians can look for success in new relationships. The position of Venus this week heralds a positive flood of new suitors on the market and Aquarians should have little difficulty in finding themselves well matched. How about that!"

Sam's eyes widened. "You mean Bill Looney might be the new love in my life?"

"Maybe."

"I don't know. I like Bill, but I can't see us as a couple."

"Maybe it'll be somebody else, then. Maybe somebody you meet at the popcorn counter tonight."

"Did you say a positive flood of new suitors?"

"Absolutely."

"Let me see that."

"You better fix your eyes, first. You've smeared your mascara."

Sam looked in the mirror and dabbed underneath her eye with a tissue. "As a matter of fact, I don't really want a new romance," she said. "I don't want to go through this again. I think I ought to concentrate on other areas of my life and forget boys. Nobody could be more perfect for me than Pip and all that led to was heartbreak."

"What are you going to do with that flood of new suitors?"

"They'll be good for my morale."

They heard the doorbell ring downstairs. "There they are," said Marcy. "Let's go."

Sam's dad was standing in the foyer talking to the boys when Sam and Marcy came downstairs.

"If you hear anything, let me know," Sam's father was saying. "You're sure you didn't recognize the voice that gave you the tip, Luke?"

"I think he was talking through a sock or something," said Luke

"It was a boy, then?"

"I couldn't say," said Luke, shrugging. "Might have been a girl."

Sam and Marcy hesitated on the stairs and looked at each other. The committee's investigation into the affair of the missing goat was obviously continuing. Sam wondered if it were wise to leave her father alone all evening. What if he got some weird desire to wash the garbage cans or clean out the garage?

"Gosh, Sam, you look beautiful," said Bill. "We'll have her back on time, Mr. Morrison. You can count on that." Bill extended his elbow for Sam to hold on

to and before she had had the time to consider plead-
ing a sudden headache so she could stay home to keep
an eye on her father, Bill had escorted her out the front
door. Luke and Marcy followed them to the car.

"Hey, what are you two gossiping about back
there?" asked Bill.

"That Nashua mascot," Luke said. "We're wondering if they'll catch the kids who did it."

Bill smacked his fist against his palm. "Not a
chance," he said. "And do you know why? Because
the whole Rebel football team is in on it, that's why."

"No kidding!" said Marcy.

"Fact," said Bill. "They move him from one guy's
house to another guy's house every couple of days. It's
like those shortwave operators in World War II that
were always moving their operations so they couldn't
be caught. The trick is you just keep that sucker moving."

Luke opened the car door for Marcy and she got in.
"Then you figure we ought to be cruising the streets
looking for a car with a goat in it," he said.

"No way!" said Bill, sliding into the back seat. "We
don't want those guys caught, do we? Nope, we want
to clobber those Nashua suckers tomorrow night and
this is the way to do it." He punched Marcy's shoulder a bit. "Right, Marcy?"

Marcy jumped a little at his touch. "Oh, absolutely," she said.

Bill leaned back in his seat and made a futile at-
tempt to stretch his legs out. "Mental attitude is
everything in a game, let me tell you," he said. "And

like it said in the *Traveler* today, Nashua's morale is shot. That was a real good article, Luke, even if it did quote those shrinks and stuff like that. What I say is, even a stopped clock is right two times a day and I guess it isn't any different with shrinks. But the point is even if Nashua got that goat back it wouldn't make any difference and you want me to tell you why?''

"Uh, why?" asked Sam.

Bill punched her gently on her arm. "Because they don't have any passing game and they don't have any speed, that's why. But when you look at our boys, what do you see? Sullivan, he's got one heck of an arm and Tracy—he's fast and he can catch." He held up two fingers. "Double trouble for Nashua."

"We're sure to win, then," suggested Sam.

"Well, I'm not saying they aren't going to put up a good fight. It ought to be a good game. Do you think you'd like to go to it, Sam?" He looked at her hopefully.

"I'm not sure," she said. "I may have to baby-sit tomorrow night."

"Oh, sure," he said, looking so depressed that she felt ashamed of herself. But truly, she thought, she did not think she could sit through an entire game with Bill. She was already practically black-and-blue from the way he was punching her tonight. If she were sitting next to him when Fenterville scored, she could end up with fractured ribs.

When they arrived at the new Ribault theater it was a blaze of light. The glass-fronted lobby with its chandeliers and the dramatic red-carpeted staircase leading to the mezzanine looked like a ballroom.

"Ho, boy," said Bill. "Look at that mob in there. That's going to be some line for the popcorn."

An usher, standing stiffly in his gold-frogged uniform, took their tickets as they went in.

"We better get in the popcorn line right away," said Bill. "Miss, are you the end of the line?"

"No, buddy, *we're* the end of the line," said a tall boy in a purple-and-orange letter sweater.

"Hey, Deever, it's that girl again," said another boy.

Sam tried to smile at the clutch of boys in Nashua sweaters. "Hi, there," she said. "Are you all ready for the game tomorrow?"

"We'll be ready as soon as we get Grogan back," growled one of them. "And we've got a secret weapon that's going to help us."

"How interesting," gulped Sam.

Looking across the lobby, Pip saw the crowd of purple-and-orange letter sweaters and suddenly froze.

"What's the matter?" asked Happy. "Have you slipped a contact lens?"

"It's Sam," said Pip. "She's over there by the popcorn machine."

Happy raised her hand to check her hair. "Is she? Maybe we should go over and say hello."

"Don't be an idiot," Pip said sharply. "Can't you see she's practically surrounded by all those guys in purple-and-orange letter sweaters. I wonder what's going on?"

"Just possibly," drawled Happy, annoyed at Pip's tone, "they are sucked in by that sweet, innocent act of hers and are standing in line to kiss the hem of her skirt."

Pip frowned. "Can't you see that she might be in trouble? I wonder if it would just make things worse if I go over there. I wish I could hear what they're saying." Now that a gap had opened between two of the garish letter sweaters, he could see that Sam seemed to be smiling. "I think she's trying to bluff them," he said. It looked to him as though one of the Nashua boys was taking something shiny out of his pocket but he couldn't make out what it was.

"Our secret weapon is this infrared flashlight, see?" the boy was telling Sam as he produced a flashlight from his pocket. "The guys that took him don't know that Grogan's coat was painted with this special dye we got from the police department. Anybody that touches Grogan gets the dye on their fingers and it won't come off for weeks. But they don't know that, see? It doesn't show up until we shine the infrared light on it." He switched the flashlight on and it glowed with a baleful red light that seemed to Sam to be reflected in his eyes. "Maybe we could sort of test it on you," he said.

"Sure," she said. "But I don't see how that would test it. I mean you'd have to test it on somebody who actually had the dye on them, wouldn't you?"

The boy shone the flashlight on Sam's fingers. As she turned her hands over under the light, the Nashua boys exchanged regretful glances.

"You weren't really thinking you'd find any of that dye on Sam, were you?" asked Luke. He had taken care to thrust his own hands in his pockets.

"Nah," said one of the boys. "We just brought the flashlight along just in case we run up against anybody who smells like a goat." He laughed.

Even though Pip was not close enough to hear anything of what was going on, he kept straining to see, hoping he would be able to tell if Sam was in any real difficulty. "They don't look exactly mad or anything," he said, frowning. "That short guy is laughing."

Happy followed his glance. "I don't think they suspect a thing," she said.

"Oh, they *suspect* all right," said Pip grimly. "The question is can they do anything about it?"

"They'd have to catch her with it first," said Happy.

Pip looked at her sharply. "Catch her with what?"

"Why, the goat, of course."

"How did you know Sam had the goat?"

Happy smiled sweetly. "You just told me," she said.

"For Pete's sake, lower your voice," said Pip sharply. "Do you want everybody to hear you?"

"Certainly not. I am a loyal Rebel fan. I support the goat heist."

Pip exhaled. "That's right," he said. "Of course you do. I guess I'm just a little jumpy lately." Again he stared across the lobby. "It looks like she's with some guy," he said darkly. He watched as a curly haired boy put his hand on Sam's shoulder and inclined his head toward her. He was saying something. Then Sam and Marcy moved off together, pushed through the swinging doors to the theater and disappeared from Pip's view. He let out a sigh of relief. At least Sam was clear of those Nashua guys.

"What I don't understand," Happy said, "is why, if you are so *deeply* concerned with Sam's welfare, you aren't going to this movie with her instead of me?"

"It was all a terrible mistake," said Pip gloomily.

"Why, thank you very much."

"I didn't mean it that way, Happy. Nothing against you. I just mean I should have never let Sam go. I'm crazy about her."

Happy moved close to him until he could smell her exotic perfume. He regarded her uncomfortably as she trailed a perfectly manicured fingernail down the front of his sweater. "I think she might take you back," she said.

"You think so?"

"You don't want to rush things," she said. "And you'll want to speak to her in person. I wouldn't try to make up over the phone."

"No," said Pip. "No, you're right. I think I'll just go over to her house and talk to her." Reeling from the smell of Happy's perfume, he was reminded of how Sam's hair always smelled clean, as if she washed it in the shower. He was already imagining how he would take Sam in his arms and beg her to forgive him for being such a jerk. His yearning to be with her was so strong it was like physical pain.

"You might want to wait until after the big game," said Happy. "She'll have a lot on her mind until then, with the goat and all."

"Keep your voice down," he implored her. "If anybody hears about that goat we could be in the soup."

"I'm practically whispering already."

"That's good. Just keep it up. In fact, let's just drop this subject, okay? Everybody and his brother seems to be here tonight."

Happy whispered directly into his ear, "Where are they keeping the goat? Isn't it kind of a problem to hide him?"

"He's in Sam's garage," said Pip, his face darkening as he remembered that awful afternoon in the garage. He could see it all so clearly now. He had frightened Sam. He hadn't respected her feelings. And maybe his irrational jealousy of Sam's friendship with Luke had goaded him, too. He had been frustrated, his feelings had been hurt, but the long and the short of it was that he had acted like a fool. Now all he wanted was to apologize to Sam and make it right with her. Belatedly he became aware that Happy was talking to him.

"I said, 'Are you ready to go on in?'" Happy asked, enunciating each syllable precisely. "I suppose you didn't hear me the first two times I said it."

"Uh, sure. Sorry. Let's go."

Happy was so angry she could feel blood vessels expanding dangerously in her head. Pip had not only scorned her, he had misled her. After all, he had been practically drooling on her when he asked her out at school and then at the pizza shop he had readily agreed to see her again. She had him eating out of the palm of her hand. No wonder she had confidently called six girls and told them about her new romance. A fine idiot she would look now, with Pip trailing back to Sam.

But she knew better than to show her anger. Already a new plan was forming in her mind and it was one that required Pip to trust her. If he had any idea of her true motives, he might go right home and call Sam tonight and that could ruin everything.

On the other aisle of the theater, Marcy and Sam had already taken their seats. "Good grief," she whispered to Sam. "My heart practically stopped back there. I thought for sure they had us. How did you get the dye off your hands?"

"There never was any dye," said Sam scornfully. "They were just trying to get me rattled so I would give myself away."

"Well, got me rattled all right. I was rattling like a tambourine. I couldn't get out of that light fast enough. And all the time I kept wondering why you were so cool. That's amazing that you saw through them. How did you figure out that it was just a scam?"

"I guess my recent experiences have made me cynical," said Sam. "After all, why did they keep explaining to us how it worked? If they really thought we had the dye on our hands, they would have tried to sneak up on us with the light." She twisted around in her seat. "It sure is taking the boys a while to get that popcorn, isn't it?" Then she spotted Happy and Pip sitting five rows back on the other aisle. The sight hit her in the face like a bucket of cold water. She felt suddenly breathless with grief.

The house lights dimmed, then went out, and a moment later Bill and Luke groped their way to the seats, bearing popcorn and cold drinks. Luke climbed over Sam's knees to sit beside Marcy and Bill took the empty seat on the aisle next to Sam. In the flickering light of the screen, Sam could see Bill's round face and his curly hair. He had all the good qualities of a friendly puppy, but she knew he was not for her. After a moment, he reached for her hand and held it in his.

No, I can't take it, she thought. This is the worst. She hardly knew what the movie was about. She sat holding Bill's hand and thinking of Pip, her throat constricted in pain. If love doesn't last forever, she thought miserably, what is the point of it?

She was not sure that even yet she understood what had gone wrong between her and Pip. Maybe it had been her fault. She knew she had never been swept away with passion the way people were in movies when music played and the camera went into soft focus. Maybe it was perfectly understandable that Pip would go looking for a more passionate person. Happy wasn't what he needed, but he would have no way of knowing that.

Or maybe the answer was even simpler. Maybe she had only persuaded herself that Pip had loved her. It was just possible that when he said "I love you," he meant something more along the lines of "Let's party."

Certainly she was going to be more careful before falling in love again. She would be like one of those divorced women her mother knew who carefully checked out whether a man helped out in the kitchen, before getting involved. It was obvious that she needed to work on becoming more tough. Hard, even. Anything would be better than sitting in the dark like this swallowing her tears.

When at last the movie was over and the house lights went on again, Sam was in no hurry to get up. She was especially careful not to look behind her. She didn't want to risk seeing Happy and Pip. Most especially she did not want to risk running into the two of them outside in the lobby.

"That's my kind of movie," said Bill.

"Ooops," said Sam. "My purse. Can you reach it, Bill?" She gave it a surreptitious kick that sent it skidding two rows down. By the time Bill was able to retrieve her purse, the theater was half empty. When they went outside, a number of cars had already driven out of the parking lot.

"Tell you what," Bill said. "How'd you all like to go over to my house and I'll cook us some fresh doughnuts?"

"You know how to cook?" said Sam, impressed.

"I know how to cook doughnuts," said Bill. "I fry them in deep fat, then I put lots of powdered sugar on them and sometimes I dip them in whipped cream."

That sounded good to Sam. She had to admit she was getting awfully tired of chili.

"What are we waiting for?" said Luke stepping on the gas.

Pip did not take Happy anywhere after the movie. Instead he drove her directly home and turned his car toward Sam's house. When he got to Mulberry Street, he stared at the blank windows of the house disbelievingly. The whole place was dark. He remembered that Sam's mother would still be out of town, and he supposed her father must be out for the evening, too. And as for Sam, she must have stopped by someplace with her friends. There was certainly an explanation for the house being dark, but it gave him no comfort. Looking at the empty windows filled Pip with a deep feeling of loneliness and longing. He felt as if Sam should have realized how much he needed her and come to meet him. He stared at the house for some time before he got back into his car and drove away.

Meanwhile Happy was in her bedroom dialing the number of Pete Mullins, Nashua's quarterback.

"Pete?" she said. "This is Happy. I have some information I feel sure you'll be interested in." She smiled into the telephone receiver.

Chapter Eight

When Sam heard the doorbell ring the next morning, she ran to the door, hoping it would be Pip. Fruity ran after her, his nails clicking on the floorboards and his ears flapping. When she threw open the door, she was surprised to find herself facing a crowd of boys in orange-and-purple sweaters. Fruity took one look at them and let loose with a full-throated howl.

"We want to see Sam Morrison," one of the boys said, raising his voice to be heard over Fruity's baying. "Where is he?"

"I'm Sam Morrison. Hush, Fruity!"

"*You're* Sam Morrison?"

"But you're a girl," she heard someone protest. "I thought Sam Morrison was a boy."

"Maybe this is the girl Deever was telling us about, the one he saw trying to kidnap Grogan."

"Yeah."

"We came to get our goat," one of the boys said pugnaciously.

Fruity, not liking the boy's tone, uttered a growl low in his throat.

"There's no goat in here," said Sam. "If you want to come in and look around the house, it's okay with me."

"Forget the house. Go out back, Mike," someone said. "Happy said they were hiding him in the garage."

Startled, Sam stepped back suddenly and landed on Fruity's tail. He let out a yelp. The boys streamed off the front porch and quickly fanned out toward the garage.

Sam stooped down and put her arms around Fruity. "Pip turned us in," she whispered. "How could he do that?"

Fruity licked her face. A moment later Sam saw the boys leading Grogan up the driveway.

"And don't think you're getting away with this, either," one of the boys yelled at her. "You're going to pay for it. And how!"

"Grogan likes carrots," Sam called after them. "He's used to having some carrots every day."

They didn't seem to hear her. There was a great slamming of car doors as the boys piled in their cars

and drove away. Once they were gone, the silence of
the house seemed to crush her. Her first thought was
of Luke and Marcy. They had to know about this right
away.

Driving over to Marcy's, Sam tried not to think
about the consequences of what had happened. She
tried not to think at all. It hurt too much.

As she approached the garage apartment, she saw
that Marcy was coming down the front steps carrying
two wastebaskets. Sam waved her arm out the window desperately. Marcy put down the wastebaskets
and came out to the car.

"They've got Grogan back," Sam said.

Marcy paled. "Oh, no. How much do they know?"

"Probably everything," said Sam, her voice break-
ing a little.

"Hang on a minute," said Marcy. "Let me go tell
Mom we're going out. We can't talk here."

A moment later she came back out and jumped into
Sam's car. "All right," she said, as they drove off.
"Tell me the worst."

Sam found she couldn't speak. The worst, after all,
was that Pip didn't love her anymore.

"That bad, huh?" Marcy said finally. "What happened? Did the police come? What did your father
say? Has he called your mother yet?"

Sam's heart sank as she realized that all these un-
pleasant interviews were still ahead of her. "Dad has
gone fishing so he doesn't know yet, but I expect it's
just a matter of time until everybody knows. The last
thing those Nashua boys yelled before they drove away

was that I better not think I was going to get away with it."

"That doesn't sound good."

Sam looked steadfastly ahead at the road. "Happy is the one who sent them. I heard them say that."

"Pip told her then. There's no other way she could have found out."

"Why would he do that to me?" Sam said wretchedly.

"I guess it's only a matter of time now until they rake us all in," said Marcy.

Sam was dismally aware that it was she who had brought this disaster on the heads of her friends by confiding in Pip. She managed a watery smile. "And just when my horoscope was looking so good, too."

Marcy colored. "Actually, Sam, I have a confession to make about that. I made up that horoscope. I was trying to cheer you up."

"You made it up?"

"Yes, the real one said something about this being a good week to make a profit selling clippings from your herb garden, which didn't seem all that helpful. I hope you aren't too mad at me. I was only trying to figure out a way to get you in a decent frame of mind for the date with Bill."

"I'm not mad," said Sam, suddenly misty-eyed. "I'm just lucky I have friends like you who care about me. I am such an idiot."

"You're not an idiot, Sam."

"Oh, yes, I am. I trusted Pip but, well, it doesn't matter. It's over. I'm just sorry that I may be bringing you and Luke down with me."

"We shouldn't have gotten you into it. You never wanted to do it in the first place."

A gloomy silence reigned.

When they got to Luke's house his mother answered the door. "Hi, Sam, Marcy," she said. "How's that investigation of the goat theft coming, Sam? I felt so sorry for Larry getting stuck on that committee. I was only glad it wasn't me. I loathe working on committees and that one was the worst."

"This was sort of a no-win situation for him," agreed Sam, thinking of how her father was going to feel when the truth came out.

"My sentiments exactly. How can you establish a good relationship with your students, I ask myself, if they know you're informing on them? Luke! Marcy and Sam are here!"

The moment Luke saw them, he knew that something was wrong.

"Let me get my jacket," he said.

While they drove to Wendy's, Sam filled Luke in on what had happened. "It's blown up in our faces," she concluded dismally. "Now we'll all get suspended, my father will ground me for good and you won't be editor of the newspaper anymore."

"Cheer us up a little, will you, Sam?" he said.

"I don't think you get credit for tests you miss when you're suspended," said Marcy in an uncertain voice. "I guess there goes my grade point average."

"Let's face it," said Sam, "it's bad. Very bad. There's no sense in closing our eyes to that. From now on I'm facing reality. No more horoscopes, no more voodoo, just bleak, cold reality."

"Okay, it's bad. But there are things we can do," said Luke. "We've got to contain the damage. Now take Marcy, for example. Marcy's got deniability. We can keep her out of it altogether. It's just Happy's word against ours and Marcy has a very clean record. She's never been in trouble before."

"For that matter, you can stay out of it, too, Luke," said Sam. "I'm the only one who was actually caught with the goods."

"Not on your life. I insist on sharing the honor of this heist. This noble exploit will go down in the annals of Lee High and I want to be a part of it."

"What about being kicked off the newspaper staff?"

He shrugged. "I'm not sure I want to be editor anymore," he said.

Sam knew he was lying, but she appreciated his insistence on standing at her side. Luke had his faults, but nobody could say he was disloyal.

"I think I should be in on it, too," said Marcy in a small voice.

"No," said Luke. "We're counting on basking in the reflected glow when you're valedictorian so you've got to keep your nose clean."

Marcy looked a little ashamed but at the same time relieved.

"Okay," said Luke, "the next thing we do about containing the damage is that Sam doesn't go home the rest of the day."

"How will that help?" asked Sam.

"You just said you were going to get grounded, didn't you? Well, you don't want to get grounded before the game tonight, do you?"

Sam could see the reasoning behind that. So the three friends spent the afternoon at Marcy's eating potato chips and playing cards while on Mulberry Street, the phone rang and rang in Sam's empty house.

When Sam and Marcy and Luke arrived at the game that night the stands were packed and the noise was incredible. Each side of the crowded stadium seemed to be competing with the other to see who could yell the loudest.

"Yo, Sam!" yelled Reggie. Sam looked up and saw him poised on the edge of a bleacher seat. "What's this I hear about you and a certain goat, huh?" he called.

Luke cupped his hands and shouted up at Reggie, "She's an authentic heroine of our time, Reg old boy."

"We shouldn't have come," Sam muttered uncomfortably.

"Why not?" said Luke. "We're going to get the static all right. Might as well get the good stuff, too."

"Hey, Sam, way to go!" some boys called out.

Feeling stupid, Sam sketched a little curtsy in their direction. She was glad to find a seat, at last, where she could sit down and feel less conspicuous. Someone jabbed her in the ribs and she jumped. "Hey, Sam!"

said Bill. He was squeezing in next to her. "You didn't have to baby-sit after all, huh? Well, heck, I knew you wouldn't want to miss this game after all you did to help out the side." He gave her a broad wink then began speaking in a confidential tone. "I guess you thought I was some kind of dope the way I was going on about the goat snatching, huh?"

"Oh, no," said Sam. "I thought it was a very good theory, Bill."

"It was all wrong, though. I have to hand it to you, Sam, you kept your lips zipped the whole time. If I have a secret, I'll know just the lady to trust with it."

Sam managed a weak smile. She was miserably conscious that she deserved no awards for keeping secrets.

She spotted Grogan tied up over by the Nashua cheerleaders. A couple of muscular boys were sitting nearby guarding him, their arms folded menacingly. On the field the players were trotting out one by one to the accompaniment of cheers.

"Look at that, will you?" Bill exclaimed. "Tracy is limping!"

Sam vaguely remembered that Tracy was one of their valuable players so she knew that was a serious problem. In the game that followed, events soon showed exactly how serious. Every advance the Rebels mounted was promptly pushed back by the Nashua team.

"What a disaster," groaned Bill. "If they could just get their defense together. And if they could just get some push in that offense, too." At last the first half came to an end and the band began marching onto the field.

"Excuse me," said a skinny girl, as she firmly stepped on Sam's instep. She squeezed past, squashing her hot dog up against Sam's jacket as her cold drink sloshed over on Sam's shoes. Sam was trying to scrub spattered mustard off her jacket when she heard Reggie calling her name. He was climbing down from the heights of the bleachers, his girlfriend Yolanda in tow. "Just too bad you didn't hang on to that goat, Sam," he said. "It might have helped us some." He bent so close to her she could smell onions on his breath. "Have you seen Pip, yet."

Sam could feel her face flaming. "N-no," she finally choked out. "It's no use. It's over, Reg."

"I'm just saying the man's been trying to get up with you. He called me up this afternoon and asked me if you were out of town."

"It doesn't matter," said Sam in a stifled voice.

"Sam, hon, don't go cutting off your nose to spite your face, okay?" he said.

Yolanda tugged at him. "Come on, Reg. Are we going to get something to eat, or what?"

"You listen to what I'm saying, Sam."

Sam could scarcely believe the force of the black emotion that enveloped her as the game progressed, the Rebels getting soundly trounced by the Nashua Wildcats. Not that she cared about the 30-0 score.

It was hard even now for her to believe in Pip's treachery. Why should he betray her to Happy? It was so much easier to think that Happy had tricked him somehow.

"I ought to have left at halftime," said Bill. "This is awful. No way can they pull out of this. What a massacre!"

Sam morosely hunched her shoulders and agreed that it was terrible.

At last the final second of the game ticked off the scoreboard and all around them fans began jumping up to surge onto the field. Bill and Sam sat disconsolately on the bleacher. "I knew it was all over when I saw Tracy limping onto the field," Bill sighed. He pounded Sam on the back. "Don't let it get you down so much, Sam. We'll have other games. And heck, it's only football."

She looked up at him. "Bill, do you know anything about truth serum?"

"What?"

"Yo!" said Luke, staggering up with his arm around Marcy. "Which way to the wake?"

"Want to go get some pizza?" Bill suggested.

"I think I'd better get on home, Bill," Sam said.

"Sure," he said. "Sure. Me, too." He looked disappointed.

"There is no joy in Mudville tonight," intoned Marcy as the three friends made their way toward the exits.

"Marcy, do you know anything about truth serum?" Sam asked. "I mean, does it really work and is there a way to get it anywhere around here?"

"You mean sodium pentothal? That's the drug they call truth serum, but it's just an anesthetic. This idea that it makes a person tell the truth has no basis in fact. It's just a myth that they use in spy stories."

"I was afraid of that," sighed Sam.

The more she looked unblinkingly at reality the worse she felt. So far, from all she could tell, hard reality didn't have much to recommend it.

When they got to Sam's house, all the lights were on inside and Sam's father's car was in the driveway.

"Do you think your father knows, yet?" asked Luke, eying the house.

"I think so," said Sam. All those lights could mean only one thing. Right now, something else was bothering her father more than the high cost of electricity.

"I'll come in with you," said Luke, "and sort of explain. After all, kidnapping Grogan was my idea."

"No," said Sam. "You've got to face your own parents. I'll manage things here."

She fumbled with her key.

Her father was sitting in the living room waiting for her. The look he gave her told her everything she needed to know.

"Did you catch a lot of fish?" she asked tentatively.

"Fish are not exactly high on my list of concerns right now, Samantha. Do you have any explanation to offer of why Nashua's goat was found in our garage?"

Sam thought for a minute. "Well, actually, I kidnapped him. Luke helped me."

"I daresay. Oh, I can believe it of Luke all right." He leaped out of the chair and began pacing up and down in front of the fireplace in agitation. "I hope I am not an unreasonable person, Samantha, and I understand that young people can be tempted to play pranks, but what I cannot understand is how you could put me in this absolutely untenable position. How do you think it makes me look now that it turns out my own daughter stole that goat?"

Sam regarded him anxiously.

"It makes me look like an imbecile," he shouted. "That's how it makes me look. What do you imagine Mr. Hendley thinks of a teacher who doesn't even have any influence on his own family? Do you think Coach Brown even believes that I could have a goat in my garage for over a week without realizing it? Why, I can hardly believe it myself! I wouldn't be surprised if he thinks I'm some sort of accomplice."

"I'm sorry," said Sam in a small voice.

"It's too late for sorry, now, isn't it?"

He ran his fingers through his hair desperately. "I'm only glad your mother is flying in tomorrow. I am so angry right now that I can't even tell what is reasonable anymore. When I think of the way you kept carrying out the garbage all week, the way you were so suddenly anxious to go out and get my tool chest! I just cannot believe you would do this to me, Samantha. I thought I could trust you. Quite obviously, I was wrong."

Sam looked down at the rug.

"Don't you have anything to say for yourself?"

"No," she choked. "I am such an idiot."

"I shudder to think that next year you'll be off at college making your own decisions. Do you think that what you've done was the act of a mature adult? Do you? Now, now, you don't have to fall to pieces over it, Sam. Stop crying. It wasn't the smartest thing in the world to do, but I guess we'll survive somehow." He stared gloomily at the mantelpiece, evidently unable to imagine anything more cheerful to say. "You'd better go upstairs and wash your face."

Sam was halfway up the stairs when her father called after her. "Pip called. I told him he'd better wait till tomorrow to call back."

Sam ran the rest of the way up the stairs, plunged recklessly into her bedroom and threw herself on the bed sobbing. Her regret for the embarrassment she had caused her father was so mixed up with her misery about Pip that she could not even be sure what she was crying about.

Chapter Nine

Sunday dawned bleak with only the thinnest of autumn sunshine sifting in through the bedroom window. When Sam got up and looked in her mirror, it seemed to her that her puffy and red-rimmed eyes reflected the state of her soul. She pulled on a bathrobe, stepped into slippers and went downstairs, hoping that a jolt of caffeine would somehow keep her going.

Her father was sitting at the kitchen table with a cup of coffee. He regarded the editorial page of the paper with undisguised gloom. For an awful second, Sam had the nightmarish feeling that her escapade had made the Raleigh paper, but a moment's reflection assured her this was a panic response.

"I have talked to Mr. Hendley," said her father. "Mr. Hendley has talked to Mr. Perkins. Coach Brown has talked to Mr. Hendley. Mr. Cummings has talked to Mr. Hendley. Everyone has talked to everyone. I am sure you'll be relieved to know that Nashua has no thought of pressing criminal charges."

"That's good," said Sam.

Her father returned his eyes to the newspaper. "The feeling seems to be that throwing you off the newspaper staff and giving you a few days in-school suspension will be punishment enough."

"It's all settled then? That's what they're going to do?"

"You'll still be called in to talk to Mr. Hendley, of course."

"Right. For the lecture."

"I don't like your tone, Samantha. True, stealing a goat is not murder, but I don't want to minimize it, either."

"No," sighed Sam.

Her father leaned his head wearily on his hand. "I hate coming across as the heavy father, Sam. You know that. Why did you have to put me in this fix?"

"It's hard to explain," said Sam.

"Try me."

"Well, after this year, we'll all be splitting up, going in different directions. Luke wanted to steal the goat so he could get a big story for the newspaper, and I wanted to be a part of it all. It was a kind of togetherness thing."

"If Luke jumped off a cliff, would you jump off a cliff, too?" He banged his fist on the table. "I can't believe I said that. That's what my mother used to say. Okay, but the basic principle is sound. You need to learn to think for yourself. Where are you going to end up if you can't make independent judgments?"

"My judgment is okay," Sam said. "It's my feelings that are out of whack. I'm not sure I want to grow up."

"Evidently," said her father dryly. "You say this was a 'togetherness' thing. Am I to assume that Marcy was in on it, too?"

Sam looked at him in alarm. She realized now she shouldn't have said that thing about "togetherness." She shouldn't have said anything at all. Now she might have given Marcy away.

"Don't have a fit, Sam. I'm not going to turn her in. In my opinion, Marcy's got enough problems without being raked in for goat thievery. And it's easy enough to see how she got pulled into this thing. She's absolutely besotted over Luke. I've never seen such a bad case. I must admit I can't see where that's going to end. Those two are so different."

He gave Sam a searching look, but she was careful to say nothing else about Marcy. She had given away enough secrets.

"Pip came by the house this morning," her father said. "But I told him I was letting you sleep in late. I hope you're not going to tell me Pip was in on stealing the goat."

"No."

"Of course not." Sam could not figure out why that should make her father look even more gloomy but it did. She supposed it got him down to think that Pip's parents had done a better job of childrearing than he had.

"So Pip came by the house, huh? How did he look?"

"What do you mean 'how did he look'? Is he supposed to look different?"

Sam turned away to run some water into the coffeepot. "I was just a little surprised that he came by, that's all. Pip and I are sort of finished."

"Maybe he doesn't know it yet," said her father, a humorous glint in his eye. "He seemed awfully anxious to see you. I told him I was letting you sleep in and that I didn't know when you'd be up."

"Well, we are kaput. Quite kaput." Sam ladled some coffee into the basket of the pot. "As a matter of fact, he's been going out with Happy."

"It's good to date a variety of people before you settle down," said her father.

"Oh, yes."

"I've always thought this business of going steady so young is a mistake."

"I agree," said Sam. "Also, I wouldn't go out with Pip Byron again if he were literally the last boy on this miserable earth." She took a few shuddering breaths, then plugged in the percolator. "I guess you're going to ground me, huh?"

He folded the paper. "No, Sam. I think it's time you started acting like an adult and taking responsibilities

for your own actions. If you want to go around town
carousing and getting into trouble, help yourself. Go
ahead. I have to drive over to Raleigh to pick your
mother up at the airport this evening. I trust that when
I get back I won't find you in jail.''

"It's only that if I'm not grounded I may try to
catch up with Luke and Marcy. We have a lot to talk
about."

"Ah, yes," said her father. "The crime. The punishment. But how do you know that *they* aren't
grounded? No, that was stupid of me. Marcy's in the
clear, officially, right? And what would be the point
of grounding Luke? He's hopeless. I suppose Eloise
and Carl gave up on controlling him long ago."

After breakfast Sam waited for her father to leave
the kitchen, then she dialed Luke's number. "Let's go
out for hamburgers tonight," she said. "I would do
anything, literally anything, to get out of the reach of
my father's reproachful eyes."

"I'll have to see. If I can, I'll pick you and Marcy
up about six. But I don't know if I'm going to be able
to get away. Things are pretty vicious around here
right now. I called Mr. Perkins and turned myself in
first thing this morning."

"What did he say?"

"Unprintable. Hey, I've gotta go, Sam. My mother's yelling at me again."

"Bye."

Sam ran downstairs. "Dad, I'm going over to
Marcy's." She pulled on her jacket.

"You don't want to stay here and listen to me berate you some more?" said her father, rattling the paper. "You astonish me."

"Maybe when I get back," said Sam nervously.

The apartment Marcy and her mother lived in might not be the last word in cheerfulness or comfort, Sam reflected as she drove over there, but at least no one there was ceaselessly asking themselves "where did I go wrong?" More than anything her father had said, it was the melancholy in his voice that got her down. She had disappointed her father. She was going to be suspended and thrown off the paper. And she had lost Pip. This was not exactly a high point in her life.

Marcy greeted her at the door with exclamations of surprise and anxious glances over her shoulder.

"Sam! Neat. Why don't you come on in my room and we can, uh, play cards or something. That was some game, wasn't it?"

But as soon as Marcy closed the bedroom door behind them, the artificial perkiness left her and she sagged onto her bed as if her bones had melted. "Oh, Sam," she moaned, "I feel awful letting you and Luke take the rap."

"Don't worry about it, Marce. What would be the point in you getting brought down with us?"

Marcy glanced at the door apprehensively. "Nobody seems to have a clue that I was in on it so far."

"The only way they got Luke was he turned himself in," said Sam. "I guess I was the only one Happy actually fingered by name."

"She'll be editor of the paper, now, I suppose you realize," Marcy said bitterly. "It's just what she's always wanted and now she's got it."

"It won't matter to me. I won't be around. They're throwing me off the staff."

"Oh, Sam, I can't stand it. I wish that instead of helping Luke with the goat I had tried to talk him out of it. You know how much being editor means to him!"

"He should have thought of that before he stole Grogan. Besides, you know that nobody can talk Luke out of anything. It's time he started acting like an adult and taking responsibility for his actions."

Marcy looked at her in astonishment. "He is! He turned himself in, didn't he? What more do you want?"

"I guess I was sort of talking to myself," admitted Sam. "I was the one who should have said no. Without my garage, he might not have been able to take the goat."

"Well, it's past praying for, now," said Marcy.

Sam sat down on the bed next to her. "When my mother gets in tonight, I'll have to go through this all again. More lectures. And then tomorrow I'll get called in to Mr. Hendley's office and lectured again. Do you think it is possible a person's health might give way under repeated lecturing?"

"I don't think so," said Marcy. "Luke's parents have been lecturing him for years and he's blooming like a peony."

"Luke says if he can get away he'll pick us up for hamburgers about six."

"Rats, I can't go. Mom and I are supposed to go over to my Aunt Hilda's for dinner. I'll have to call him and tell him. You'd better keep a close eye on him tonight, Sam. He's more upset than he let on about having to give up newspaper staff. You know it's been practically his whole life. I'm afraid he may do something desperate."

"I won't take my eyes off of him," said Sam. "If he starts to slash his wrists, I'll be on him like a ton of bricks."

Luke came by Sam's house at five. She threw on her coat and called a quick goodbye to her father.

"I thought you said six," she said as she got in the car.

"I got out while the getting was good. I guess you know Marcy's over at her dumb Aunt Hilda's. Why did Aunt Hilda have to invite them over for tonight of all nights? I am putting six ancient Parsi curses on Aunt Hilda's head."

"If you've got any spare curses," said Sam, "why not put some on Happy?"

"Wouldn't I just love to? I hope she gets hit with a major libel suit her first month as editor."

"I hope she gets fat."

"I wish her teeth would turn black," said Luke.

"I wish she'd get very fat."

"Oh, for Pete's sake, Sam, getting fat isn't the worst thing that can happen to you!"

"That's what you think."

"She's been licking her chops over being editor from the start. She's probably having a celebration right now," he said gloomily.

"She's scum."

"You said it."

"Actually, I wish she would die," Sam said.

"You really do hate her, don't you? It's Pip, isn't it? That's what's really getting to you."

"Not a bit. As a matter of fact, I wouldn't go out with Pip again if he came crawling to me on his hands and knees and begged me to."

Taking one look at her face, Luke handed her his handkerchief and Sam spent a moment sobbing into it while he tactfully looked straight ahead.

"What drives me crazy," Luke said, "is the way Happy gets away with everything."

"I know," sniffled Sam. "She's so sneaky, so conniving."

"She always gets off scot-free," Luke lamented. "No mud ever sticks to her."

"Why don't we pool our allowances and have a contract taken out on her?"

"Oh, I don't know if I actually want her dead or anything—the blood and gore, the guilt. I just wish she'd move away or something. Seriously. Hey, wait a minute, Sam! I've got an idea!"

Sam blew her nose and looked at him hopefully. For once, Luke's saying "I've got an idea" rang no warning bells in her mind. The pain she was feeling was so burning that Sam was sure she could have fried an egg on her heart, and she was eager for distraction.

"Listen," Luke said, "let's at least show her just how we feel about her for once. Let's put a hundred For Sale signs on her lawn."

"I love it! But where would we get a hundred For Sale signs?"

"The town's full of them."

"I don't think we could get a hundred in the car."

"So we can do it in shifts. I've got all night. My parents are driving over to a wedding in Winston-Salem. They won't miss me. Anyway, maybe we don't need a hundred. Just a *lot*. Is your dad expecting you home?"

"He's got to go all the way to the Raleigh-Durham airport to get Mom. He's going to be gone for hours."

"All *right*!"

When Sam's father went to answer the doorbell he found Pip standing there.

"Is Sam home?" asked Pip.

"She's gone out for hamburgers with Luke. I'm sorry you seem to keep missing her, Pip. They left about five and I expected them back by now, but they didn't say when exactly."

"Do you think I could just wait?"

"Well, you could ordinarily, but you see I'm just about to go pick up Sam's mother at the airport outside of Raleigh." He was about to close the door, but something in Pip's look made him add, "I suppose you could wait here while I'm gone. I don't see why not."

"Thanks," said Pip simply. He came into the living room and lowered himself into the chair by the fireplace. He looked out the window and noticed for the first time that it was already quite dark. "I guess Marcy was with them, huh?"

"No, I don't think so."

Pip stared at the empty fireplace in silence.

"I've got to be going now, Pip. There are some magazines under the coffee table over there if you want them."

Pip heard the back door close and a moment later heard Mr. Morrison's car backing out of the driveway.

He turned on the lamp by the easy chair and forced himself to pick up a battered copy of *Field and Stream*. Gritting his teeth in determination, he began reading it.

The wind blew through Sam's hair as she stuck her head out the window of Luke's car. "There's another one!" she cried. "And it's a good one." The best targets were houses with unmowed lawns and a neglected air, where the For Sale signs could be snatched in perfect safety. But even taking signs from inhabited houses where the windows blazed with light was not at all difficult. The signs were out by the road and usually the stakes weren't pounded very deeply into the ground.

Luke slammed on the brakes and they got out. Sam helped him wrest the Blake Realty sign out of the sod and they piled it in the trunk on top of the other signs they had collected.

"I think the trunk is just about full," said Sam. As they slammed it closed she had heard the sound of cracking wood as one of the stakes splintered.

"You're right," he said. "We've got enough."

They jumped back in the car and Sam turned on the radio. "Sticking them up in Happy's yard is going to be a little bit trickier."

"Piece of cake. Don't worry. Bet you the whole family's in the back somewhere glued to the television. It'll be easy. Hey, are you hungry yet?"

"Starving."

"Why don't we go by and get something to eat before we swing over in that direction."

Singing along with the radio in a passable baritone, Luke drove to a nearby Burger King. His arm was resting on the open window and to Sam he looked completely carefree. There was no doubt about it. Stealing For Sale signs was therapeutic. Sam felt better than she had in days. Luke pulled into the Burger King parking lot.

"Yo, Lancaster!"

Sam's head snapped to the left when she heard Reggie's voice. Splat. Luke swore as a stream of water landed square on his nose.

Sam could hear Reg cackling as he gunned his engine and swerved out of the lot. His arm was hanging out the window and he was waving a red water pistol.

"I'm going to get him," said Luke. He gripped the steering wheel tightly as they careened over the speed bumps following Reg. "Open the glove compartment."

Baffled, Sam opened the glove compartment. A couple of plastic water pistols lay on the stack of maps.

"Are they loaded?" Luke asked. He had not taken his eyes from Reggie's tail pipe. They were close behind him, roaring down Sunset Avenue.

Sam squinted at one of the pistols. "I think they're full," she said.

"We've got to conserve our ammo. Don't fire until you see the whites of his eyes."

Suddenly Reggie turned into the parking lot of Spinnaker Cove Apartments.

"We've got him now," whooped Luke.

Reggie began circling the lot. Luke lay in wait for him by the Dumpster and as Reg's car drew parallel to theirs, Sam stuck her hand out the window and fired a stream of water at Reg.

"I got him!" Sam shrieked. "I got him."

"Ho-ho," Reg yelped, speeding down the lot.

"Gimme," said Luke, holding out his hand.

"No, you've got to drive. I'll do the shooting."

The two cars pursued each other around the parking lot again and again, Sam shooting sometimes with both pistols at once. "Hey, take it easy," Luke yelled at her. "Don't waste that water." She got six solid hits, which she thought was pretty good, but Reg was no mean shot either and her hair was getting pretty wet.

"We're going to need a refill pretty soon," Sam yelled at Luke as he tore to the far end of the parking lot. "Do you see a hose anywhere?"

"There's a spare under the seat," Luke said. "But give it to me. I haven't had a chance yet."

Sam groped under the seat and produced another water gun.

"Reg and I have a sort of running game," explained Luke. "So I try to keep an extra one in reserve."

She handed over the spare water gun.

Luke flourished it out the window and yelled "Geronimo!"

In his excitement, he bumped the car up on the curb and Sam heard a telltale explosive sound.

"There goes the tire," said Sam.

"Hey, Reggie! Truce!" yelled Luke. "We've got a flat."

Reggie's only response was a splat of water on their windshield.

Luke's car was listing badly. He swore under his breath. "I'm going to have to change it. Come on, Sam, help me."

"Help you change the tire? I don't know how to change a tire!"

"Help me get at the spare. It's in the trunk under all those signs."

Reggie scored a direct hit on her bottom when she bent to lift a sign out of the trunk. She yelped in surprise. "No, fair, Reg. We're disabled."

"Hey, man, all's fair in love and war," yodeled Reggie, waving his water gun. But then he drew his car up beside them and watched with some interest as they began unloading the For Sale signs from the car and stacking them on the sidewalk. "What's up?" he asked.

"It's a surprise for Happy," Sam explained, pulling another sign out of the trunk.

Reggie's eyes opened wide. "She's for sale? Hey, what makes you think anybody would buy?"

Sam laughed. It seemed like ages since she had felt like laughing. She would have to get a pair of water pistols herself now that she saw their rich potential. She pushed her damp hair away from her face, then watched in surprise as Reggie's car glided swiftly away. In a matter of seconds he was out of the parking lot and gone without having even said goodbye, which was not like him.

When Sam turned around, she suddenly understood why Reggie had departed so quickly. A police car was entering the parking lot from the south, its blue light blinking.

"Okay," Luke panted. "I'm down to the tire."

"Don't bother," said Sam. "I don't think we're going to need it."

"Oh, jeez," said Luke softly when he spotted the cops. "I guess we were making too much noise. The neighbors must have called them."

A huge man in a blue uniform got out of the police car and walked deliberately up to them. "Can I see your driver's license?" he said.

Sam gulped. She had suddenly remembered that her father had expressed the hope that she would not be in jail when he returned.

Luke's blue eyes were fixed on the policeman's face with a look of intense sincerity. Sam supposed he hoped in this way to keep the policeman from noticing the heap of For Sale signs on the sidewalk. She could have told him it was no use. The parking lot was well lit and it wasn't as if they were inconspicuous. Who had ever seen so many For Sale signs in one heap before? "We were just trying to change our tire, officer," said Luke. He held out his license.

"You don't have to worry about that tire right now, son," said the police officer. "We're going to be giving you a ride." He motioned toward the police car.

There was a metal grille between the back seat of the police car and the front seat. A two-way radio in the front seat made crackling noises. Sam sat in the back seat next to Luke, shivering. She hadn't paid much attention before to how wet she had gotten but now she realized that not only were strands of wet hair hanging in her face, but there was a distinctly cold spot on her rear where Reg had scored his direct hit. Nobody said very much as they drove to the station.

Sam was relieved when they arrived that nobody produced handcuffs.

"In there," said the cop, nodding toward the door.

She could feel herself shrinking as she imagined getting fingerprinted. She had the idea that they also photographed you from two unflattering angles. You had a number hung around your neck or something.

She remembered seeing that in the movies. Reluctantly they moved inside.

"Sit down," said the police officer.

A line of polished wood chairs was pushed against the wall opposite what looked like a dispatcher's desk. Sam sank into one of them and Luke sat down beside her. They sat on the hard chairs for some minutes.

"Not exactly a gabby bunch, are they," muttered Luke.

A policeman glared at him.

Two police officers came through the door with a man who was staggering and mouthing obscenities. His face was shiny and his eyes rolled wildly. Blood was running down his face from a cut on his forehead. Sam noticed his handcuffs and shuddered as the police shoved him down the hall.

"Okay, kids," said the officer who had brought them in. "Call your parents to come pick you up."

Sam and Luke looked at each other in horror.

"Uh, officer," said Luke. "My parents are away."

The policeman smiled. "Don't worry about it. I expect we can find some place for you to stay. A cell or something like that."

Luke jabbed Sam in the ribs. "Call your parents, Sam," he whispered.

"I told you my father had to drive to Raleigh."

"What are we going to do?"

Sam looked at her watch doubtfully. "I guess they might be home by now, if they didn't stop for dinner." She rose. "Uh, officer, if I don't get any answer, do I get another phone call, or do I just get one call?''

"Oh, I think we can let you have more than one call," said the policeman.

"If I can't get Mom and Dad," Sam told Luke, "I'll call Marcy. Her mother would bail us out."

"Aunt Hilda, remember? They're over there tonight."

"Don't you remember Aunt Hilda's last name?"

"Why would I know Aunt Hilda's last name? It's not like Aunt Hilda and me are bosom buddies."

"Maybe Mom and Dad will be home," said Sam, her voice trembling a bit. She was not sure what she would do if they were not.

The police officer led her to a phone in a nearby hallway and then stood away from her. Watching him out of the corner of her eye, Sam dialed her home phone number. To her relief, after the seventh ring, she heard someone picking up the phone.

"Hello?"

"Pip!"

"Sam!" he cried, "Where are you? You were supposed to be home ages ago. I've been going crazy worrying about you."

"I need to talk to Daddy."

"He's at the airport. I thought you knew that. The flight must have come in late or something. Where are you?"

"At the police station," Sam said softly.

"I can hardly hear you. Did you say at the police station?"

"It's a long story, but they won't let us go unless our parents come and get us. I think they may lock us up."

"Good Lord, Sam, what did you do?"

"Nothing. Nothing much, that is. Luke and I just had a flat tire and we had to take out all these For Sale signs out of the trunk to get to the spare."

"Why would the police care about that?"

Sam eyed the policeman doubtfully and lowered her voice still more. "I guess they weren't exactly our For Sale signs," she admitted. "We were going around getting them off people's lawns. What am I going to do? I don't want to spend the night in jail. When do you think Dad is going to be home?"

"It could be a while. You know what it is with these delayed flights. It can be hours. Look, Sam, hang on. I'm going to take care of it."

"You can't take care of it. We've got to get hold of our parents. That's what the police officer said. And when we said we might not be able to reach them, that's when he started talking about jail."

"Hang on, Sam. Nobody's going to put you in jail. I'll be there in a minute."

"But Pip—"

"I'll bring my mother. She can fix it."

"No! Don't do that!" she cried. But he had already hung up.

Chapter Ten

It's our policy to release them to the parents," the man at the desk said.

"I understand that," said Pip's mother. "But since we can't reach their parents right now, I will be personally responsible for them." She smiled at the police officer. "They aren't bad kids. Don't you think you have given them enough of a scare?" She drew off her kid gloves to reveal a diamond as big as the Ritz.

It was evident to Sam from the beginning that Mrs. Byron was going to have no trouble with the police officer. Sam was not sure whether this was because of her quiet confidence, her charming smile—so unnervingly reminiscent of Pip—or her position as wife of Fenterville's foremost citizen and major employer.

The policeman commented, as Mrs. Byron was signing for their release, that his first job had been sweeping the floor of one of the Byron tobacco plants, which might have been a clue to what counted most with him.

Moments later Luke and Sam followed Pip and his mother out to their car. The night air was growing chill. "The police in this country are so courteous," Mrs. Byron was saying. Pip's mother did not have a strong accent. Only the quality of certain vowels betrayed her Spanish origins.

"How did you get wet?" Pip asked Sam.

"Water pistol fight," Sam replied.

"A water pistol fight?" Pip repeated, smiling. He liked the idea of a water pistol fight. It seemed like the farthest thing from a make-out party. Luke's glittering good looks had always made Pip feel awkward and ungainly by comparison and never more than now when he felt so unsure of Sam. It bothered him a lot that she kept refusing to meet his eyes.

Luke and Sam climbed into the back seat of the shiny car and Pip got into the front seat, though with reluctance. He would have preferred to be back near Sam.

"I didn't like to ask any questions since I thought the sooner we got out of there the better, but I am not sure I followed exactly what the police officer was saying about For Sale signs," said Pip's mother, inserting the key in the ignition.

"It sort of loses something in the translation," Sam said lamely. "We were collecting For Sale signs. It was a joke."

"Those guys back there didn't seem to have much of a sense of humor," said Pip.

"I don't believe they ever had any intention of charging you with anything," put in Pip's mother. "They were only trying to frighten you."

Sam shivered. "If that was what they were after, they succeeded beyond their wildest dreams."

"Where can I let you off, Luke?" asked Mrs. Byron.

"I guess you'd better drop me off at Spinnaker Cove," Luke said.

"Not home?"

"I have to pick up my car."

"All right. But please don't get into any more trouble tonight. I did tell the policeman I'd be responsible for you."

Luke's car was sitting in the parking lot of the apartment complex just where they left it, but the huge stack of For Sale signs had disappeared, confiscated by the police.

"Need any help with that tire?" Pip asked Luke as they let him out.

"I'll manage," said Luke.

Pip got in the back seat with Sam, but still she did not look at him. She seemed deeply interested in checking out the Dumpster.

"Sam, I think you should go back to our house with us until your parents return," Mrs. Byron said as they drove off. "I don't like to think of you waiting in that big house alone."

"Oh, I'll be fine," said Sam.

"I'll stay with her," Pip said.

They had spoken simultaneously. Stopping suddenly, they looked at each other and then Sam quickly looked away. She was distressed at how strong her feeling for Pip was, even after all that had happened. Why did he have to come rushing to her rescue? Why couldn't he just move away somewhere, preferably Siberia, so she didn't have to see him anymore? She should have put those For Sale signs on his lawn.

"I'm not sure the Morrisons would like that arrangement, Pip," said his mother. "Why don't we just see if they are home and if they are not, Sam can come back with us."

When they got to Sam's house, there was no sign of Sam's father's car, but she jumped out of the car anyway. "They'll be home pretty soon," she said. "Thank you so much, Mrs. Byron. I'll be fine now."

Pip had already gotten out the other door, ignoring his mother's protests. He followed Sam up the front steps and stood close to her as she unlocked the door.

"Go away," she said. She was having trouble with the key and Pip finally took it from her and opened the door for her. "Quit *rescuing* me," she said venomously. "I hate it."

He followed her into the house and closed the door behind him.

"I told you to go away," she said.

"So, call the police."

"Oh, *you*," she raged.

"Look, I'm sorry, Sam. What can I say? I'm really, really sorry."

"How could you tell her?" Sam asked, groping wildly in her purse for a handkerchief.

"Tell who? My mother? How else was I going to get her to come to the station? She didn't think anything about it, Sam. You know she likes you. She figured it was all Luke's doing and that you were more or less an innocent bystander."

"Not your mother—Happy. Why did you have to tell Happy?"

"Tell Happy what? I don't know what you're talking about."

"You know what! You told Happy about Grogan."

"The goat?"

"Yes! The goat. Are you going to pretend you don't know anything about it? Those guys told me that Happy let them know where he was. How else could she find out except from you?"

"What guys?" asked Pip, looking bewildered.

"All those Nashua football guys. A bunch of them showed up here yesterday morning and took the goat back and now Luke and I are going to get suspended and thrown off the newspaper and I hope you're satisfied." She blew her nose loudly.

"Sam, it was a mistake. God, I'm sorry. It just slipped out before I knew it. She saw how upset I got at the movie the other night when those Nashua guys ganged up around you and she guessed what was up

But I never figured she was going to tell anybody. She acted as if she was on our side. Are you sure she was the one who told?''

"Those guys told me right out that it was Happy. It's just the kind of thing she'd do. If you knew her a little bit better you'd see that. You two deserve each other.''

"Oh, come on.''

"I *trusted* you. I was an idiot.''

"I'm sorry, Sam. I don't know how it happened. When I saw you surrounded by all those purple-and-orange sweaters I just about went nuts.''

In spite of her anger, Sam was beginning to have some idea of how Pip could have accidentally let the incriminating information slip out. It was difficult to watch your tongue when you were upset. Hadn't she unintentionally given Marcy away when she was talking to her father? She looked at him from under her lashes, seeing him blurred through the prisms of her tears. "You were worried about me, huh?''

"I was scared out of my mind.''

"I bluffed them. I was pretty good.''

"I'm sorry I wasn't as good as you,'' he said remorsefully. "If I'd kept my mouth shut you could have pulled it off.''

Sam burst out laughing. "If you could just hear yourself, Pip. It sounds like you wish you were in on it.''

"I do wish I was in on it,'' he said. He put his arms around her and she didn't push him away. "I miss you, Sam. I didn't know about the goat, but I've been thinking about that other stuff a lot and I can see that I was acting like a jerk. I wasn't trying hard enough to see your side of it. Heck, I was so steamed up I didn't know what I was doing."

"No, I should have seen your point of view more, too," sniffled Sam, wiping her eyes with the back of her hand.

"Don't start that. You'll get me all confused. I had it all set in my mind that I wasn't going to push you anymore. We'd just go to, uh, concerts and things. You know, events of cultural interest. Whatever you want to do. How would that be?"

"You really mean that?"

"I hope so. I mean, I can't say it turns me on a whole bunch, but the last week hasn't been any picnic, either."

Fruity pawed at Pip's pant leg.

"He hates to be left out," Sam said, "when people are hugging."

Pip bent down to scratch his head. "He still remembers me."

"Well, you haven't been away that long."

"Seems like forever." He straightened up and pulled her toward him, pressing her close to him to kiss her. Sam heard the back door opening and started to giggle. "It's the folks."

"Hey, stop that," said Pip. "We don't have much time here."

"Sam!" her father's voice called from the back of the house. "We're home."

Sam didn't answer, her mouth was hungrily pressed to Pip's.

"Sam!" called her mother.

Fruity trotted off to the kitchen to greet them.

Sam reached under Pip's shirt and began caressing the small of his back.

"Hey, watch it," he hissed. "They're coming in here."

When Sam's mom and dad came into the room, Sam and Pip were trying not to look like two people hastily disentangled from an embrace.

"Pip!" said Sam's father, not looking very pleased. "Are you still here?"

"We just got here!" Pip said.

"Sam, your hair is all wet!" said her mother. "Have you been outside like that? You'll catch your death of cold. Come in the kitchen where it's warmer. I've got some snapshots of the baby. I think he has Robin's eyes."

"If you just got here," frowned Sam's dad, clinging stubbornly to the original subject, "where have you been?"

Sam looked uneasily at Pip. "I was out running around town with Luke and we sort of got raked in by the police."

"Sam!" roared her father.

"What were you raked in for?" asked her mother.

"We were just playing a little joke. Nobody got hurt and they didn't charge us or anything and Mrs. Byron came up and got us."

Sam's father was pressing his hand to his forehead with an anguished expression.

"Now remember what we were saying in the car, Larry," Sam's mother said.

"I know. You're only young once. I remember. But Ginny, this is too much. The police!"

"Maybe we ought to hear Sam's story before we start screaming at her," her mother said.

Sam felt a rush of warmth toward her mother. She hadn't realized how much she missed her mother's steadiness, her reasonable voice, her hot-buttered corn bread. "We really didn't do anything so awful," Sam said.

"I guess I'd better shove off, huh?" said Pip. He squeezed Sam's hand. "See you, Sam."

Sam's eyes followed him as he moved out the door. She hated to let him out of her sight.

After Sam had finished hashing out the evening's events with her parents and had managed to convince them that criminal charges were not pending, she called Marcy and told her that she and Pip were reconciled.

"So you're back together," Marcy said.

"Can you believe it?"

"Sam, you're going to break up eventually. He's probably going to go to some school far away and those long-distance romances never work out. Why not just get it over with?"

"We're all going to die eventually, too. But that doesn't mean I want to do it now."

"What are you going to do about this sex thing?"

"I don't know. I'm going to take it as it comes, let it unfold, be true to my feelings."

"That is a prescription for disaster, if you ask me. Can't you see you could end up ruining your life? Weren't you listening when I told you that was how my mother ruined her life? I don't care how gone you are on Pip, you ought to be able to see that the two of you come from different worlds and that in the long run this is never going to work."

"You are such a snob, Marcy. Just because Pip's family has money that doesn't make him any different from anybody else."

"Oh, yes it does. Besides, I could make a list a mile long. You and Pip are different in every conceivable way."

"Not true," said Sam. "Our hearts are the same."

"I give up! You are such a romantic there's no hope for you at all."

"I know you're upset because Luke is getting kicked down from being editor, Marce, but nothing you say can bother me tonight. I have stainless-steel happiness. I don't know what it is, but Pip and I have something. There's this tenderness—I don't know. It's always been that way with us. It wouldn't surprise me if we loved each other for a long, long time."

"It would me," said Marcy. "And remember, this is the guy you hated only yesterday. But I'm not going to say any more, Sam. If this is what you want, I'm very happy for you."

"You don't sound very happy." It occurred to her that Marcy was probably not capable of experiencing the simple happiness that she felt tonight. Marcy was complex, with the sort of ambition that kept her up nights glued to a calculus book when any reasonable person would prefer to be watching a late show. Pip had that, too. It was odd, she thought, that of the three or four Morehead scholars that would be nominated from her school this year, two of them would be the two people closest to her. She thought about pointing out this amazing fact to Marcy, but decided against it. For one thing, she had the feeling that finding out Pip had a grade point average to rival her own would not improve Marcy's already bad mood. That single-mindedness about achievement that Marcy and Pip shared was something Sam couldn't fully understand, but she accepted it. She liked them just the way they were—a little preoccupied, a little intense, a little different from her.

"I'm still feeling awful about letting you and Luke take the rap alone, to tell you the truth. If only I weren't afraid it would affect my grade point average—I've just got to be valedictorian, Sam. You know how it is. It's winner take all. The valedictorian gets a whole smorgasbord of scholarships and the runner-up gets zip. You understand, don't you?"

"Sure, Marce. Don't lose sleep over it." Sam felt like embracing the entire world. She wished she could beam some of her happiness to Marcy over the phone wire. "You're being too hard on yourself," she said gently. "You've got a little problem that way, you know."

Sam heard a tapping noise on her window and almost dropped the phone, but when she peered anxiously at the pane, she could make out Pip's face.

"Gotta go, Marcy," she said. "Pip's at the window."

"At the window? The window of your bedroom? Oh, good grief!"

Sam dropped the receiver onto its cradle and went over to throw the window open. "What are you doing up here," she whispered. He threw a leg over the sill.

"I came to see you. What do you think?"

"Shhh," she said, looking anxiously over her shoulder as he climbed inside. The cold draft was making the curtains billow inward and Sam quickly closed the window behind him.

"Luke's not the only one who can do crazy things," Pip said with satisfaction.

"I don't want you to be like Luke! I like you just the way you are!"

"Come on, Sam, you *love* me just the way I am, don't you?"

"All right, I love you," she said nervously. "But that doesn't commit me to anything." She could imagine the scene if her father happened to stick his head in the room to check on her. Arrested by the police and caught with a boy in her bedroom on the same day! She'd never recover from it. She darted an anxious glance at the window, wondering if the neighbors had seen him come in. "You could have broken your neck if you had fallen off the roof," she said.

Pip sat down on her cedar chest. "I'll bet I called you a hundred times yesterday and today. I've been trying so long to catch up with you I just wasn't ready to leave just now when your parents started giving you a hard time. I mean, we just got back together! What are they going to do? Ground you for the rest of your natural life?"

Sam made a face. "Worse. They are going to treat me like a mature adult and make me feel guilty."

"Who were you talking to when I came in?"

"Marcy."

"She's delighted we're back together, I guess."

"Of course," said Sam. Sam sat down next to him on the chest. She wondered if this craving that she had to be close to Pip, to touch him, was a sign of an immature relationship or something like that.

"I've been thinking about what you said," he began. "You know, about the future? Do you remember when you said that riding a camel and watching the sun rise over the Pacific were biggies for you?"

Sam nodded.

"It just gave me this cold feeling. It's hard to explain. I could tell you had this picture in your mind, this vision, you know, and I was thinking Where am I in that picture? I can't see you alone, Sam, you're not the type. Don't kill me for saying that. I know you keep saying you're independent and all, but you're not a loner. You can't deny that. So I started thinking about how some other guy was probably going to be with you and I wanted to kill him."

Sam smiled.

"Okay, I didn't say this was going to sound intelligent, right? It's just this feeling that I had. I was thinking it's going to be tough if it comes to that."

Sam leaned her forehead against his shoulder and thought about how she had told Marcy that they had the same heart. It was true, she thought.

"Sam, I just want to put my arms around you and never let go."

They sat for a moment with their arms around each other feeling unaccountably sad. Sam wiped her eyes with her sleeve. "This is dumb," she said. "We should be happy. We're back together, aren't we?"

"I know. And I've got to get home and do my calculus. I haven't gotten a blinking thing done in days. If I don't get moving my grades are going on the skids for sure. I threw the window screen down on the ground, by the way. I think it'll look as if it just fell out."

The mention of the screen brought Sam back to reality with a crash. Her parents would be coming upstairs to go to bed any minute.

"You'd better go," she said. "I really love having you here but if my father caught you in here, believe me, he would not understand."

"Heck, I don't understand it myself." Pip grinned.

Sam lifted the window and peered anxiously out at the dark roof, outlined at the far edge by the streetlight. "Oh, be careful," she said. "Don't break your neck."

"I won't," he said, climbing over the sash. He turned to blow her a kiss. "Sam, I love you."

"I know," she said. She smiled as she watched him scramble over the roof and lower himself to the edge. As he dropped to the ground, Fruity let out a howl of alarm.

She heard her father swearing in the hall outside. "He's been like that the whole time you've been gone, Ginny," he was shouting. "We're going to have to get that dog some tranquilizers or something. I can't stand it anymore."

Sam lowered the blinds and pulled the curtains closed. She wondered why she had been driving herself crazy thinking about the future. "I love you." That was more than enough, she thought. For now.

* * * * *

Will graduation mean the end of the In Crowd? Find out next month in SO LONG, HIGH SCHOOL, *from Keepsake.*

COMING NEXT MONTH
FROM
Keepsake

KEEPSAKE # 37
ALABAMA NIGHTS
by Brenda Cole

With all her heart, Stacy wanted to live on the farm near the boy she loved. But her mother didn't agree. Who was right?

KEEPSAKE # 38
SO LONG, SENIOR YEAR
by Janice Harrell

Saying goodbye to Lee High is a bittersweet experience for the In Crowd.

AVAILABLE NOW

KEEPSAKE # 35
JUST LIKE JESSICA
Judith Blackwell

KEEPSAKE # 36
YOUR DAILY HOROSCOPE
Janice Harrell
#3 of *The In Crowd*

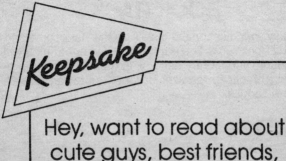